ALL WE ARE **SAYING**

ALL WE ARE SAYING

BY

S.T. STETKA

This is a work of fiction. Any resemblance to actual events or persons, living or dead, is entirely coincidental.

First Edition: 2022

ISBN 978-163972564-9

ststetka@gmail.com

Order Online at Lulu.com

A Native American grandfather was talking to his grandson about how he felt.

He said, "I feel as if I have two wolves in my heart.

One wolf is the vengeful, angry, violent one.

The other wolf is the loving, compassionate one."

The grandson asked him, "Which will win the fight in your heart?"

The grandfather answered, "The one I feed."

- *Black Hawk*

This was a framed saying that hung in the mud room of the Clarke house, at kid height, ever since I can remember.

CONTENTS

INTRODUCTION

We fast forward to the year 2082. It is November in Washington, D.C., and preparation is underway for its participation in the Worldwide Observance Celebrating the 50th Anniversary of Peace, and how what seemed to be, in the blink of an eye, the world started its turn, swiftly and surely, into the New Age.

A Golden Anniversary, remembering a time when we were moved by a comforting force so abundant, it spread like a large warm blanket, sheltering all and resulting in an unforeseen shift into a collective compassion that benefited everyone, everywhere. Holding no more attraction, aggression, manipulation, and denial fell by the wayside, dwindled, and expired.

An old man being interviewed about his memories of that time said, "Peace?" with a question mark. "Why, fifty years ago when Peace started, it was only, after-the-fact, that we saw how much lip-service we paid to pretend we were all working for it. Back then, even those of us who believed in the Peace Movement, we all thought we were right, but we didn't have a clue about how it could happen or the way it did or on the scale. There really wasn't anyone who thought it would happen, not like it did."

One of those who witnessed the changes, first-hand, was Odell Davis. Now 77, she has shared her early memories from 2012 to 2033. She was a close friend, and an integral part of the inner ensemble of people that helped usher in the New Age, and this is her story.

FIFTY YEARS AGO

In 2032, the world and its problems had been the same, and mostly worse since the turn of the century. I was 27, living in Washington, D.C. and working for a top political media analyst company. I thought I got the job because I had a great education, but I was, and had been for twenty years, best friends with the now sitting "First Family." I had known them, their friends, and close political associates, since I was seven. So self-inflation aside, I certainly was hired because I knew and had people.

In a few days, President Clarke was up for re-election, and for a lot of reasons, everyone knew that he was a sure win. There wasn't any drama or political stammering. On that day, I was waiting for a phone call from his daughter, Janie, my best friend, to let me know if I was going to be invited to re-election night at the White House with her and her family. My boss wanted to know, as he was counting on me being there. He was calling and asking, "Have you heard from her yet?"

I told him, "She's got a lot on her plate, she'll call when she knows."

My boss called again, "Have you heard? Are you coming in?"

I told him, "No and yes," watched some news, and headed to work.

I wasn't there five minutes when he called me into his office and asked, "What are you going to do today?"

I said, "Well I'm just waiting to hear."

He said, "Not good enough. If you don't get asked to the White House, we don't have a story. So, this I what I want you to do. Go to your office, close the door, put your feet up, block everybody but her, and think about it, remember what you can. You've known them for how long? Twenty years? Do it chronologically. See if there's a pattern. Take your time, all day or until you hear from her."

I went back to my office, did what he said, closed my eyes, went back in time, and thought, "Wow, twenty years is a long time."

THE FIRST TEN YEARS

In 2012, I was seven when my parents moved from D.C. to the suburbs of Northern Virginia. They never wanted to leave their beloved inner city, but they knew that they had to get me off the ups and downs of elevator life from a fifth-floor, 650 square foot condo. With promises of kids and yards we approached the move. It was an early August evening, cool and misty, and we were doing the final walkthrough for closing the next day. We came out of the house with our agent. My parents were excited. Everything was going smoothly. She was remindi [illegible] them about what they needed to bring, whe [illegible] looked over to the house next door. Three [illegible] were coming out the front door and our ag [illegible] "Those are the people I told you about."

My mother asked, "Congressman John Clarke? Is that him and his wife?"

"Yes, and they're closing tomorrow too."

As they continued to talk, I looked over and the man looked back at me. He smiled and waved. He flashed the peace sign and pointed at me. I smiled. He pulled on his jacket, pointed at me, and flashed the peace sign again. I was trying to look down at my jacket when my mother tapped me on my shoulder, made me turn my head, and gave me the other kind of peace sign, the one that's upside down, where it goes from her eyes to my eyes. "Odell, honey, focus, did you hear what she said? [illegible]e people next door, they're going to be our [illegible] and they have a girl your age."

[illegible]houted over to the other agent and [illegible] meet and greet on the sidewalk. [illegible]ne, smiling. She was beautiful. [illegible] her waist, and she rested her [illegible]hey seemed just as excited as we were. My father and Mr. Clarke lamented about the lack of 24-hour flashing neon or a place to get a beer close by. My mother and Mrs. Clarke talked about moving day, sharing contacts, kids, and school. As they were winding it up, Mr. Clarke got down at my level, looked at me, smiled, gave me the peace sign again and pointed to my jacket. When I pulled up on my jacket, I saw it had peace signs all over it. I laughed. He then rolled back the corner of his jacket lapel. There was a big plastic button and when he pushed it, it lit up like a pinball machine, and blinked a multi-colored peace sign. I said to him, "That's silly."

He smiled and said, "It's not silly, you just have to give it a chance." Then he pointed to my jacket again, I looked down and he came up with his finger and plinked me on my nose and we both laughed.

Our car floated all the way home to our condo that night. I sat on a cloud in the back seat, while my mother beamed with joy about their decision and our new neighbors.

On moving day, my father had to work, so my mother and I were at the new house waiting for the truck to come. The Clarkes were moving in on the same day. Mr. Clarke wasn't going to be there for the move either, and their two kids, a boy nine and a girl seven, were off with their grandparents on vacation. I remember my mother talking to my father about three o'clock in the afternoon and saying, "I can't believe how much stuff we have. The movers next door have already come and gone over two hours ago!" We had boxes everywhere, when Mrs. Clarke called and invited us over. Wanting to see their house and needing a break, my mother and I made our first neighborly visit.

When Mrs. Clarke opened the front door, my mother's eyes bugged out. Everything was in its place, most of the artwork up on the walls, and not a box in sight. Mrs. Clarke showed us around. She was even nicer than I remembered. In the family room there were already pictures on the mantle. Mrs. Clarke pointed out their wedding picture, their kids. There was a military picture of a young man. My mother looked at it and questioned, "Is that your husband?"

She said, "No, that's his brother, his half-brother. He was older and died in the last days of Vietnam. He was only there for a week when he was killed. John was just seven." She looked at my mother and said solemnly, "John and his parents never recovered. John still has nightmares and none of them talk about it." She then pointed out more pictures and said, "Now, this is John with me in college, where we met; and this is David, he and I went all the way through school together and then onto college, best friends; and this fellow in the background over here, that's Hal, Henry Allen Lee, but we call him Hal. He's John's top political adviser, tough guy. We were all close in college. David used to work with John as an ethics adviser, but became a spiritual counsellor with his church, after getting disillusioned with politics."

She then led us out to this enormous, enclosed porch that ran the whole length of the back of their house and said laughingly, "Now this is the real reason we bought this house. We love having parties. Sometimes we have a small band, people sing, the kids run around, and this porch is going to work out just perfect!"

As Mrs. Clarke and my mother walked back into the house, I stood at the porch window and gazed into their backyard. The late afternoon sunshine glistened through the trees, the ground sloped slightly downward, the grass was like a big green pillow, and a winding stone walkway led to an old, weathered storage shed set perfectly in the middle of the yard. Seven-year-old visions of suburbia excitement stirred my imagination, while two squirrels chased each other across the top of a fence and onto a neighboring tree.

When I came back in, they were already in the kitchen, talking away. Mrs. Clarke was pouring wine and putting out cheese. They hit on every subject they could. Why they bought in this neighborhood? My parents bought because they liked the older homes, and it was in their price range. The Clarkes because she didn't want an oversized overpriced mega mansion. "I know he's a Congressman, but maybe not forever. I want to live within our means, and I don't want to move." And then she said, "I'm one of those it-takes-a-village people, while John is more of a world-want-to-be-guy. So, we make it work. Don't get me wrong, I love his passion and his constituents love him. The reality is, I didn't want to live in the public eye, but once the political bug got a hold of him, well, we moved here for some semblance of normalcy."

My mother liked to tell a story or two and said, "My husband and I met at a business conference in Colorado. We fell in love, got married, and we were sure we didn't want kids. A few years later we went back out west for another conference. We stopped at his favorite brewery. We were full of ourselves, drinking, talking our stuff, and before we knew it, we were thinking about having a kid. He said the only way he would is if we named it after his favorite beer. I asked him, 'Really? Whether it's a boy or a girl?' Uh huh, along she came, and the rest is history."

I remember them laughing, and as Mrs. Clarke was setting me up in the den with a snack and a big coffee table picture book, there was a little knock on the front door. When she opened it, a kid stood there and he blurted out, "I heard a boy moved here."

"Yes!" she answered, "His name is Jack, what's yours?"

"Andrew, I live right over there."

"Hi Andrew. I met your mother the other day. My name is Mrs. Clarke."

"Can he come out?"

"No, sorry, he's not here yet, he's with his grandparents, but he'll be home tomorrow." Mrs. Clarke turned, pointed to me and said, "This is the girl that just moved in next door. Do you want to say hi?"

He looked around, saw me, we both slightly waved, and he said, "No, I'll wait until tomorrow." Then he started to walk away when he tripped on his shoelaces. She tried to get him to tie them, but he refused and then he tripped again, all while backing down the walkway and saying something like, "Dang it!"

Mrs. Clarke laughed out loud and said to my mother, "He's so cute and the only boy Jack's age around here."

The conversation wasn't slowing down, but it was getting late, when the front door swung open and in walked Mr. Clarke, unexpectedly, and with a small bouquet of cut flowers. Mrs. Clarke met him in the hall with a hug and a kiss saying, "I didn't think I would see you until later tonight?"

"I'm on my way to that dinner, but I wanted to stop by for just a minute and bring you these." Looking around he said, "Wow the place looks great and so do you!"

She hugged him again and said, "Our neighbors are here." He poked his head into the kitchen and said hello.

Raising her eyebrows, my mother laughingly commented, "Flowers? Very nice!"

He said, throwing the sweetest smile, "Well, first night in our new house and the kids won't be home until tomorrow." Mrs. Clarke blew him a kiss.

I watched as she walked him to the front door, he put his arm around her waist, pulled her close and said, "Later babe."

They said their "love you" "love you too" thing, and as he walked out the door, they were met by a delivery guy with a big beautiful floral arrangement. Mrs. Clarke read the card, "To my best friends, congratulations on your new home. David."

Mr. Clarke grimaced and jokingly moaned, "Ugg, beat out by a best friend." Again, they kissed.

Later that night I told my father, "I never saw people kiss so much."

I don't remember the day I met Janie Clarke, but I do remember the first day of school, which was only a week or so away, and we were already best friends. On that morning I showed up at their house, all set for school.

There was a mud room and four cubbies, one for each of us, not just for their two kids. Andrew was fully in the mix, as Mrs. Clarke was doing for him, what she was doing for me, before and after school care. We were waiting on Andrew. Finally, we see him struggling up the sidewalk. His shirt isn't tucked in, his belt isn't buckled up, he doesn't have everything in his backpack. It looks like he's limping.

Mrs. Clarke calls out to him and tells him not to worry, plenty of time. Dishevelled he gets himself into the house. She says, "Can I help you with your belt? You don't have it in the loop."

"No, I'll get it," as he tugs away and bangs his elbow on the corner of the counter.

She said to him, "Andrew, honey, aggravation isn't good and someone's going to get hurt, it's just a matter of time." Andrew and I both spent most of our young days under Mrs. Clarke's wing. She was always saying stuff.

Mr. Clarke wasn't home so much, but when he was, and we were there, what a treat. He would walk through the door and someone would yell out, "Monster!" He would put that scary contorted look on his face and Mrs. Clarke would stand close to the hallway as he came through holding out his briefcase with one hand and pulling on his tie with the other. She would blow him a kiss, he'd respond in kind, but with a monster face, then he'd make groaning noises and start to come after us. We would scramble, pretend to hide, each of us screaming to be picked up and tossed about, all while running away. We didn't know from congressman and all of that. We just knew him from being Mr. Clarke. He'd play with us until Mrs. Clarke would call out, "Food's ready!" and we'd still be begging him for more.

Andrew always wanted to get the last of the attention. "One more time Mr. Clarke! Again!" Mr. Clarke would oblige and always tussle his hair one more time. If we were lucky, we'd play *If I Ruled the World* at the dinner table, where we'd all get to be silly and say stuff, like, if we could, we'd put gummy bears in everybody's mashed potatoes. Everyone would laugh. Good times. Kid times.

One night early on, before I headed home, Andrew's dad was coming by to pick him up. Mr. Clarke had a teleconference with his adviser Hal and was looking for some peace and quiet. When Andrew's dad came to the door, Mrs. Clarke spoke with him and then he left without Andrew. When Mr. Clarke questioned her, she whispered, "Said he'd have to take Andrew with him to a late job and he looked like he was aggravated, so I told him we were all going to watch a movie and asked him, if Andrew could stay?" Mr. Clarke didn't seem happy and when he spoke with Hal a bit later, I overheard Hal question the judgement of getting involved with a needy neighborhood kid. It's hard to explain, because I was only seven, but I already knew, for me, the Clarkes were my gravy, my sprinkles on ice cream, but for Andrew, they were his meat and potatoes, his bread and butter.

It seemed like a lifetime, when it was just a few short months, the beginning of November and the 2012 elections were coming, as was the election night party at the Clarke house. By then Mrs. Clarke and my mother had solidified their friendship and when she invited us to the party she said, "It's going to be an early evening, from six to ten, with food, drinks, and a not-to-loud live band playing sixties music on the back porch. No politics. The kids will have fun, John's parents are coming, and you can meet the people I've been telling you about. It's a good time, you'll see."

So many memories from that night. Across that long bank of windows, on the back porch, white string lights sparkled. There were new people laughing, and the smell of comfort food and cupcakes wafted through the air. The band was tuning up and us four kids were just getting wound up. Jack and Andrew went one way and Janie and I went another. As we scattered, Andrew yelled out, "Let's get this party started!"

As we were running, I tripped and almost fell into Hal. Janie told me that us kids were to call him Mr. Hal. He was a stern man and didn't appreciate the fact that any of us kids were running around. He was standing with his wife, Miss Janine, who was as stern as he was, and next to them was their twelve-year-old son Hal Jr. Jack said, "I've known him all my life and never once saw him play."

My parents were just being introduced to Mr. Clarke's parents, when the four of us kids collided in front of them. Mr. Hal came over, gruffly broke up the introductions, and wanted to know, pointing to Andrew, "Where's the parents of this kid?" Mrs. Clarke started to say, they were working and would be by later, but Mr. Hal barked, "Who sends their kid to a party like this unchaperoned?" And before Mrs. Clarke could say anymore, her father-in-law jumped in, dragged his wife in, and both sided with Mr. Hal in his complaint about how things are done nowadays.

In the middle of it, my father tried to overcome the awkward situation by showing everybody a badge he had made special for the night's festivities. It looked like a cartoon ka-pow sign with a bold jagged red outline and in the middle were the letters, **I Y W I Y.** Mr. Clarke's mother, studied it, took the bait, and asked, "What does it mean?"

My father replied in a cartoon voice, "I yam what I yam."

In some animated gesture of aversion, she rolled her eyes and moaned to her husband, "Oh no, not another jokester."

Mr. Hal butted in and addressed my father by our last name, "Davis," he said correctively, "Popeye, not the theme."

But my father, not wanting to miss a beat, resorted to an old family standby, put up his dukes and said, "I can whip any man three times my heavy and twice my old." There were confused looks in the crowd, but my mother and I laughed. My father always made us laugh.

As the night went on, every time we ran by the grandparents, they would reach out to either straighten Janie's hair or tuck in Jack's shirt and Mr. Hal and Miss Janine would admonish with they're downturned glances and subtle instructions, to either slow down or watch out. The only positive stranger in the group was David. Janie told me, "We call him Uncle David, cause he's like an uncle." He did some funny tricks, made us laugh and then chased us just enough to get us all in trouble again.

Andrew's parents finally arrived. They looked like they were having an argument when they came through the door. She was behind him and veered off to say hello to Mrs. Clarke. He bristled past Mr. Hal asking, "Where's the bar?" There was some undercurrent talk about them, but the party was in full swing and their entrance took a backseat to the busyness.

As the night went on, and the music played, Mr. Clarke took the mic to introduce a song, saying it was, "One of my brother's favorites, an early Dylan tune."

Right when he said that his father, halfway across the room, blurted out in a painful defiant tone, "That wasn't his favorite singer," and then grabbed his wife's arm to pull her into the other room, she flinched, and he yelled at her, "What? Come on!" It was noticeably harsh. Mrs. Clarke turned a little pale. Mr. Clarke put his hand up as if to shield his face, shook his head, turned away, and cued the band. As I remember it, after a couple more songs, most everybody was singing, swaying or slow dancing, even Andrew's parents. It was the end of the night and just the beginning of my life with my new neighbors, the Clarke family.

THE NEXT TEN YEARS

The first ten years went by like butter. A thousand more things could be said, but it would all be redundant. Everybody seemingly stayed the same, Mr. Hal, Miss Janine and Hal Jr., Uncle David, Mr. Clarke's parents, and us four kids, but Mrs. Clarke still had a bad feel for this political thing and Mr. Clarke was still having his nightmares.

It was 2022, late October, Janie and I were seniors, and the boys were in their second year of college. They went to different schools, but both were just a couple of hours away. The mid-term elections were coming up, and so was the election night party at the Clarke house. Despite, or because of, what Mrs. Clarke called the most caustic and divisive political arena, she announced another let's-get-along type sixties-seventies themed party. Jack and Andrew would come home, and party plans made.

I had a speech due for my Descriptive Essay Class, and it had to be about someone I knew well. I choose Mrs. Clarke because I knew everything about her. I spent the last ten years, almost every day, around her. She's an open book, not just to me but to everybody, and so I had plenty to work with.

I asked Janie if she wanted to hear some of it and she said sure. I told her, "It's just a rambling outline and starts with the word Repetition."

She laughed and said, "Duh."

And so, I started my random reading of Mrs. Clarke's repetitive quotes, "If you can't say something nice, then don't say anything. The glass is half-full. Life is good. It takes all kinds to make a world. Think before you speak. Patience is a virtue. Forgive and forget, and friends know what friends do.

"If we heard these once, we heard them a thousand times, and not to mention, her latest one from the Dali Lama, 'I do not judge the universe.'

"When we were younger, she would say, 'Without repetition you'd never learn your goesintas.' We would get that crossed look in our eyes and she would laugh saying, 'You know, two goesinta four, and three goesinta nine.'

"She's always laughing and is a natural at it. Same funny commercial, same old sitcoms, seen so many times, and she still genuinely laughs out loud. Says she got most of it; the smiles, the dated phrases, and the 'nothing-but-blue-sky' attitude, from her parents.

"Claims to have a favorite Beatle, eats Fluff from the jar, and has a tee-shirt that says:

To Be is to Do - Socrates

To Do is to Be - Aristotle

Do Be Do Be Do – Sinatra

"She loves to sing and dance and is addicted to YouTube on the big screen in the kitchen. She might not admit it, but she is. If we could recover her playlist from over the years, you would know what I'm talking about. A few years ago she played *Camila Cabello's Havana Oh Na Na*, specifically the Jimmy Fallon live version, a hundred times, always changing the words to Savannah Oh Na Na, and then say with a grin, once again, that she and Mr. Clarke spent a week one night in Savannah.

"She's fun, but she's also a very sensitive person and refuses to watch any violence, gore, or horror. She won't watch it on tv, in the news, or at the movies. She told us when she was eleven, eleven mind you, she had a bad reaction while watching the old movie, *Billy Budd.* The story goes that when they were ready to hang Billy, she went spastic and begged her parents to save him. Of course, when they couldn't save him, because it was just a movie, she lost her ability to discern reality, couldn't find her breath, started to hyperventilate, and turned blue. They had to slap her on her back to bring her out of it.

"She's a self-labelled minimalist. Hardly ever gets new stuff, saying with a smile and as a lesson to us kids, that she keeps her yearnings separate from her earnings. You can see, by what she brought into their home, when they first moved in, and the calmness it exuded, that it didn't change much. No added pomp, no circumstance, no shopping just to shop. Literally, she wears her clothes and shoes until they're done. Not that she doesn't look good, all the time, because she does, it's just that years of pictures, bear me out, showing how many times something was worn, consistently, until it could do its job no more.

"She looks to make extra time, so she can just think and told us she stopped folding towels, for that very reason and set up bins for the big clean towels and put the smaller ones in drawers in the kitchen and baths. Despite the sense it makes to me, it brought about an uneasiness and an almost visceral affront, in Mr. Clarke's mother, who criticized, 'That it just doesn't seem right.'

"She is, let's just call it quirky. She doesn't go to the hair salon because she cuts her own hair. Sometimes it comes out good, sometimes not so good; and she only washes it every five days, and bemoans that on the fifth day, it's usually at its best. She never uses soap on her face, and at the end of her shower, she always, says always, turns the water to ice cold and fully drenches herself in it. And when it comes to exercise, she cites "Arnold" and how ten repetitions fully focused is better than one hundred with a wandering mind."

I looked up from my paper and said to Janie, "That's all I have so far. I've got a lot more material, but it's not due for another two weeks, what do you think?"

She had been grinning the whole time I was reading it, "Wow," she exclaimed, "you know my mother all too well."

We both laughed and I said, "I know, right?" and then asked, "Do you think she'll like it?"

"Oh yeah, except for maybe the hair and showering thing, that's a little weird."

I responded, "You think?" and we laughed again.

Mid-term election time was upon us and the boys were home. We learned our lesson from the last party, no messing around. That year, 2020, Mrs. Clarke choose a more contemporary music theme for the party. The last song of the night was, *I Believe I Can Fly*. She orchestrated a mini flash mob similar to the Stockholm Airport version. Us kids were involved and right when the song was over, instead of dispersing, the three of us egged Andrew on and he took the microphone and sang the words from one of our long-standing favorite songs, *Welcome to the New Age, to the New Age,* then he extended his arm out to the right, intentionally dropped the mic on the floor, and walked away. The four of us loved it. We were just having some fun, but overall, it didn't sit well.

Now two years later, Mrs. Clarke reminded us about how the smallest amount of agitation can mess with people, and we were to be on our best behavior, no horsing around. We either had to help out or just be nice.

Andrew's parents weren't coming. Mr. Clarke's parents, Uncle David, Mr. Hal, and Miss Janine were there, but Hal Jr. wasn't. My parents had become party staples, attending every party they had since we moved there. My mother and Mrs. Clarke had become best of friends, confidents.

My father was over saying hello to Mr. Clarke's parents and showing off his badge for the evening. "Another ka-pow sign," he says, showing off the letters **M S P.**

Mr. Clarke's mother does her reluctant asking, "What does it mean this time?"

My father says boldly, "Mumbled Sunshine Promises."

When from behind Mr. Hal speaks over my father's shoulder and says instructively, "Such are promises..."

My father looks back and asks, "Really, you sure?"

"Yes, Davis, I'm sure. And its mumbles, not mumbled." Shaking his head, Mr. Hal asks, "What kind of guy doesn't look that up before he puts it on a badge?"

But my father was quick and blurted out, "Hey, sometimes a man hears what he wants to hear."

And Uncle David, standing within earshot, unexpectedly chimed in saying, "and disregards the rest." And like two guys full of themselves, my father and Uncle David had a good laugh. Mr. Hal and the grandparents, not so much.

Miss Janine was on her phone all night, texting, calling, sounding like she was trying to get in touch with Hal Jr. Mr. Hal stood over her and seemed to annoy her with his questions and saying things like, "You mother him too much."

She shot him a sneering look and said, "Go away."

He started back at her, talking even more, and she became even firmer, with her hand outstretched, "Go away!"

I asked Jack what he thought was going on with Hal Jr. and he said, "Word is, he's been depressed. I guess for some time, and he isn't doing too well, and they," pointing to Mr. Hal and Miss Janine, "fight about it all the time."

The night seemed long. The music lagged. There was an edge, people were tired. Mrs. Clarke was already a bit blue, when she overheard Mr. Clarke and Mr. Hal talking under their breath and saying something to the effect, "They should just throw away the key."

Mrs. Clarke stepped in and said to her husband, "Babe, I thought we agreed to let go any talk like that for tonight, at least for the party?"

Mr. Clarke looked at her and said, as if she were bothering him, "What? You don't know what we were talking about... just take it easy." And then with his hand, dismissed her and continued on with Mr. Hal.

She stumbled backwards from the sheer impact of his disregard. I think she started to cry. I had to turn away, but she recovered, and in a few minutes, she was circulating again, and the night went on.

Shortly after that, an older couple introduced themselves to Mr. Clarke's parents saying, "We heard you lost a son in Vietnam, you must be so proud of his service?"

Mr. Clarke's mother whimpered, as if she heard about her son's death for the first time, all over again. Mr. Clarke's father gathered his wife in his arms and replied belligerently, "Of course we're proud." Then called out, "We're leaving early, your mother's not feeling well."

Mr. Clarke just waved his father off and said, "Okay."

Mrs. Clarke said to her husband, "Why don't you go over and help them out. They don't seem to be doing well."

Mr. Clarke replied, "They're fine." Then let his parents leave without any more acknowledgement or affection.

Boredom started to set in, and Andrew said, "It might be the choice of music, put you to sleep." Mrs. Clarke heard him as she walked by. He said, "Sorry Mrs. Clarke, no offense."

Wearily she replied, "No offense taken."

The party was coming to an early end. The last song, *American Tune*, although great, seemed sad for 2022. When it finally ended, the four of us were standing off in a corner and without any pre-planning, we quietly sang together, *Thunder, feel the thunder, lightning and the thunder, thunder*, but we were quick about it, almost imperceptible, and then like our own mini flash mob, we dispersed.

The four of us had agreed to stick around and help clean up, when I overheard Mr. and Mrs. Clarke talking off to the side. She said, "I can't believe you spoke to me that way tonight."

He answered, as if he didn't recall, "What are you talking about?"

Which upset her even more, "You know what I'm talking about. When you slagged me off in front of Hal."

He denied it again and their conversation went quiet.

Jack and Andrew were taking a few things out to the shed when Mr. Clarke noticed they had been gone for a bit. I watched from the porch window, as Mr. Clarke went out into the backyard, down the stone walkway, peered into the shed window and caught the boys smoking some pot. An old bowling ball bag that used to be in a bucket on the floor, was now opened on the counter. Mr. Clarke was dramatic in his confrontation. He yelled pointing to the bowling bag, “Is this where you keep your stash? At my house?”

And Andrew said, “Well it really isn’t a stash.”

Mr. Clarke snapped at him and told him to, “Shut up!”

Jack started to say that it was his, but he was ordered to, “Get in the house!” When he balked, Mr. Clarke screamed, “Did you hear me? Get in the house!” Then turning his sites on Andrew, he grew colder with every word, “Go home and don’t come back. You got it? You’re done here.”

Andrew said something about being sorry and Mr. Clarke replied, “Sorry? You’re done, you got it?” And then he turned, grabbed Jack, and dragged him into the house.

It all happened so quick. From inside the house, Mrs. Clarke heard something going on but didn't grasp it in real time. Jack stormed up to his room and slammed the door. Mr. Clarke's face was beet red, and it looked like he was going to punch a wall. Ranting and raving, laying all the blame on that kid, as if Andrew was the cause of everything wrong.

With all this drama going on, Mr. and Mrs. Clarke had to pull themselves together, as they had committed to go to another election party that night, and their car was waiting. Mrs. Clarke was shaken to the core and looked like hell. Mr. Clarke was sweating profusely and talking to himself.

I had planned to sleep over that night and thought maybe I should go home, but Janie begged me to stay. Mr. and Mrs. Clarke came home later and at about four in the morning we were awakened by Mr. Clarke suffering through the worse nightmare we had ever heard. The sound coming from him was so loud and eerie, crescendoing, up and down, with a *Wooo, Wooo*, as if a ghost was being scared to death. With everything else going on, this unnerved everyone even more.

The next morning Mrs. Clarke had to be somewhere early and was gone when Andrew came over to apologize to Mr. Clarke and make mends, but Mr. Clarke turned him away saying, "It's best this way. It's over with here. Don't come back."

Mr. Clarke didn't know it, but Jack was at the top of the stairs. He heard what his father had said, packed his bag, got in his car, and left for school before his mother returned and without saying a word to anyone.

Later that day, against Mr. Clarke's wishes, Mrs. Clarke went over to Andrew's house. His father answered the door and said that Andrew went back to school too and then asked her, "What happened?" Mrs. Clarke tried to explain, but none of it came out right. Andrew's dad said, "I hope you all figure it out, that boy loves you."

Crushed, Mrs. Clarke returned home and called my mother over for some wine and commiseration. The talk went straight to her anxiety about Mr. Clarke's fight with Andrew and the intensifying nightmares.

Later that night my mother told my father, "You know, I've never seen her so distraught."

Then my father said something about Mr. Clarke that floored me. He said, "John never liked Andrew."

My mother begged to differ, "No, that's not true."

"Oh, it's true. I've known it for a long time. Maybe he didn't say it front of you women, but he said it in front of us guys."

I was in shock. How could Mr. Clarke not like Andrew? We were his other kids? I thought he loved us and this whole mess with Andrew was just a speed bump. It was a difficult reality to wrap my head around.

Despite Mr. Clarke's stand to keep Andrew away, us kids continued to communicate, and I decided not to tell Janie, Jack, or Andrew what my father had said.

That speech I had to finish for school, the fun one about Mrs. Clarke, it lost all its lustre. My tone was muffled, my inflection was off, and my voice couldn't reach the pitch of enthusiasm I had planned.

Winter Break came quick and both boys came home. Nothing had changed. If Mr. Clarke wasn't going to invite him, Andrew wasn't going to set foot in their house again. Mrs. Clarke was physically ill from the whole thing. She tried to talk with Mr. Clarke, but to no avail. One evening, just before Christmas, there was a knock on the door. Mrs. Clarke opened it and it was Andrew's mother. She looked Mrs. Clarke in the eyes and begged, "What are you doing to my son?"

Mrs. Clarke fumbled for what to say.

Andrew's mother said, "You take him in and then you throw him out?" And as she walked away, asked with tears in her eyes and her voice shaking, "What's wrong with you people?"

Mrs. Clarke was left shattered in the hall. Mr. Clarke saw her standing there and asked, "Who was it?"

She said, "Andrew's mother. She was so upset."

And with a belittling tone, he mocked, "Oh, she's so upset."

Mrs. Clarke bent over, as if a burden was too heavy.

And with an air of impertinence, Mr. Clarke added insult to injury and shouted, "What? What did I say now?"

It had become almost too painful for me to hang out at the Clarke house, but soon high school was over, Janie and I headed to college, and a few years passed. For some of us, things changed for the good, but for Mr. and Mrs. Clarke it didn't.

He seemed to get worse, mouthier. She looked downtrodden, her hair never looked right, and she always seemed at a loss for words. From a distance they showed well, but the underlayment was crumpled. Compared to what it was when we were kids, it reeked of forced smiles and picking battles. Mrs. Clarke thought something needed to be fixed and Mr. Clarke didn't.

Andrew adjusted the best he could and was always a joy to hear from and see. Jack, not so well. It tore him up and he went quiet, not just with us, but with everybody, and especially with his father.

It was Spring Break 2027. Janie and I were in New York City where we met a group of friends at an Open Mic night in Brooklyn. A friend of a friend went up and read a poem he had written, but it was more than that, it was a performance and the crowd applauded. His name was Christopher. He sat next to me at the table, and we spoke for some time. As the evening ended, he threw out an invite, saying he was having a party and free wine tasting tomorrow night at the beverage store he managed. Kind of a get together so his aunt, who is visiting from out of town, can meet some of the people who know him. I laughed and questioned, "But we just met?"

He was so nice when he asked, "Couldn't you just pretend?"

The next night Janie and I decided to go to Christopher's party, but as we were heading out the door, Janie got a call from her mother saying that tomorrow her father was going to announce his, not too unexpected, candidacy for President and he wanted her to come home. A car was being sent and a flight was booked. So, I went to the party alone.

There was a nice crowd, twenty plus people. Christopher came over to meet me as soon as I walked in. We small talked. I told him I liked his poem, especially his way of telling it, and he told me he likes people who like his poems. We laughed. It was comfortable and he was good at blending me with his friends.

His aunt was there talking with a woman. Christopher said he would introduce me after he opened a bottle of wine. I was standing close enough to overhear their conversation. The woman was saying, "But it's the law, everyone, has to participate in the Jury System."

And Christopher's aunt said, "True, but nobody can make me judge another person. I'll do jury time, if they want, but I can't be forced to judge someone."

Just then Christopher came back, worked his way into their conversation and introduced me. She was sweet, smiling, and reached out to touch his arm when she talked about him, and he made her feel special. Later he would tell me that she took him in when he was a teen and too much for his parents to handle. He said, "I used to sneak out at night with my friends, just to write poetry. I wasn't good at school, but somehow when I wrote, the words just came to me. I got great parents, but at the time, my aunt was the one who gave me the space I needed. She's cool." He laughed and said, "She's an old hippie."

Christopher and I saw each other over the next couple of days, but I had to go back to school, and it wasn't in New York City. We promised to stay in touch, and we did.

The whole "throw your hat in the presidential ring thing" with Mr. Clarke was underway. When Janie got back to school, we talked. She told me that because of her father's political aspirations, things weren't good at home. She said, "I can't believe it, we've become such a dysfunctional family. Jack doesn't call. My mother's not happy and my father's oblivious."

A few days later my mother called saying she and Mrs. Clarke got together for wine the other night, "And by the way, Mrs. Clarke says hello and hopes you're well." And then went on to update me on how she was doing. "Well, she's a mess, and from what she tells me, his nightmares are non-stop and when she asks him to open up, he tells her that it's none of her business; and if she tries to bring up the affect it's had on Jack, he loses his mind. She's afraid he's going to have a stroke. And I told her, I'm afraid you're going to have a stroke."

I asked my mother, "Do you think they'll split up?"

"Oh, I don't think so. When I ask her, she said she loves him, still looks for him at the door, and misses him when he's gone, and that she was sure he felt the same way about her. Says they love being together, but this thing about him not wanting to come to terms with whatever is bringing on the nightmares is ruining their life. And she said sometimes she finds him so aggravating that no amount of asking him to stop works. She told me that she went to David for advice."

"What did he say?"

"He told her what she already knew, until he wants to open up, there's nothing anybody can do. And then he told her, you know, sometimes couples are happy when they are young, and live with the anticipation that they will, naturally, grow closer and happier in their later years, but sometimes that doesn't happen and then he asked her if she was prepared to accept that?"

"What did she say?"

"You know how she is, a hopeless romantic, she quoted a line from one of her favorite movies and said…I choose us."

I laughed and said, "That's Mrs. Clarke." And then asked my mother, "People do change, if they want to, I mean, he could, if he wanted to?"

My mother replied, "Odell, honey, the key is, you have to want to, and this has been going on for how many years, at least since 2022, and here we are almost five years later, and they seem to fight all the time. She says it's a nice day and he says it looks like rain, never mind about this whole thing with Andrew and Mr. Clarke's father. I don't know how they're going to make it through this presidential bid."

But somehow, they did. My mother said that Mrs. Clarke had resorted to a "let it go" type of mantra and didn't speak much. I was studying overseas and not home when Mr. Clarke won the 2028 Presidential Election. I saw it on the news and none of it looked like sweet victory.

After the election we all didn't have as much communication as before, but we knew from what we did hear, that life as a First Lady only exacerbated her situation. Mrs. Clarke found that she was irritated with the enforced rigidity of her position and was suffocating in her own silence. Whether she picked her battles or said nothing at all, she ached. She felt somewhat stuck, but couldn't leave, she just wanted to be happy, to be better, and while she was thinking that Mr. Clarke was thinking something else. He wanted her to pick up her pace and to stop criticizing him, after all, he was the one elected President. And so her approaches to effect any change in his willingness to delve into whatever was causing him to carry an attitude, to hold a grudge, and to cry out at night, failed. She told my mother, "It should have been a solvable Psych 101 problem, but sadly because of the compounding of time, it's bigger than that now."

Clearly, Mr. Clarke was experiencing some ill effects, as it was wreaking havoc on his blood pressure and his stomach was always in a bind. Their time together became less, and yet, he continued to condone his flagrant unwillingness to even approach the notion of change. He used defensive statements like, "She just won't let it go.

This whole thing. What? I can't even have my own thoughts. If I don't think her way, then I'm the one who's wrong?" And so, the nightmares continued, and the impatient denials left her silently alone, instead of close to him.

Soon we were already into the second year of Mr. Clarke's Presidency and I was spending the weekend with Janie at the White House. Discussion was underway about the 2030 mid-term election party. Mrs. Clarke was desperate to have it at their "real house" as she would call it, in our old neighborhood in Northern Virginia. Desperate because she wanted Andrew to come and wanted Mr. Clarke to do the inviting. Desperate because Mr. Clarke's parents were getting old and Mr. Clarke needed to mend the wound, whatever it was, for his parent's sake, for his sake and for the sake of the family. Mr. Clarke did not want to discuss, and so their talks stalled. Mrs. Clarke decided to call Uncle David over in order to help bridge the gap.

When Uncle David arrived, Mr. Clarke accused them of an ambush. Janie and I could hear everything from the other room. Things escalated, not so much that there was fear, but more of a distant disconnect. They went back and forth, and in the end, Mr. Clarke said he would agree to invite Andrew to the party, in return for them laying off this thing with his father.

Mrs. Clarke let out a disappointing, but imploring plea to reconsider, but then Mr. Clarke screamed at her and Uncle David, "I'm tired of all this, you got it? Oh, you feel so sorry for my father, you want to know what happened? I'll tell you, but don't ever ask me about it again."

Janie and I listened through the wall as he went on, "The night before my brother left for Vietnam, he went to my father's room, across the hall from mine, it was the middle of the night. He stood in the doorway, his shadow trembled, and he told my father that he was scared. And do you know what my father said?" Then he yelled, "Do you know what he said? My father told him, 'There's no yellow in this family.' I could see my brother's body breakdown as he turned and slumped back to his room. And that was it, no other words, no comfort, and the next morning, as if nothing happened, we saluted my brother as he walked away." And with tears in his eyes Mr. Clarke cried out, "Who says that kind of thing? Who does that to someone?"

When Uncle David asked if he had ever brought it up to his father, Mr. Clarke said, "I tried once, years ago, but I couldn't get the words out, and any mention of that night and my father acts as though he doesn't have a clue."

Then Mr. Clarke stiffed up quickly and said, "I don't want to talk about it anymore. You got it? This is my decision. You want Andrew at the party, then invite him. I'll give you that, but don't tell me about my poor father! Because he isn't."

We all knew there was something bad between Mr. Clarke and his father, and now we knew what it was, and the darkness it revealed cast shade like a never-ending storm.

With only half of what she really needed emotionally, Mrs. Clarke moved forward to have the mid-term election party at their old house, and my mother heard all the plans. It was going to be in the afternoon, two to five, and she planned an outside venue with a fifteen-piece orchestra, five vocalists, and a light rock theme. There was going to be a good-sized, wider than deep, blue, and lighter-blue vertical striped tent, with three terete tops, set on a raised stage stretching all the way across the back of the yard. It's a much smaller tent, but similar, to the one in the 2006 YouTube video of Procol Harum live in Denmark. In keeping with that visual, she had the lawn chairs covered with red and white seat covers. Andrew was invited and he accepted.

Jack was going to be there. All four of us, all together, one more time at the Clarke house.

The Secret Service did a sweep of the neighborhood. The street was blocked off, there was a medical team, a swat team, a helicopter, snipers on buildings. It was intense, but we were ready, us four kids arrived right on time. My parents were on their way, but with all the traffic, would be about a half hour late. Mr. Clarke's parents were inside on the back porch and not sure they'd come out to the yard. Uncle David just arrived and was saying hello to Mrs. Clarke, Miss Janine, and Hal Jr., and was asking if he could help, but Mrs. Clarke said they had a full staff handling everything.

For the beginning of November, it was a hotter than usual day. The four of us stood in the afternoon sun with our backs to the house facing the yard. Mr. Clarke approached with Mr. Hal and with their backs to the stage and shed, they stood on the downside of the grassy slope facing up at us four. The air was thick.

Mr. Clarke didn't reach out to shake Andrew's hand. There were veiled pleasantries. Andrew had been talking about his psychology-based radio talk show project. Mrs. Clarke casually walked up and stood next to Mr. Clarke. When Andrew looked to finish his story, Mr. Clarke rolled his eyes and asked with ridicule in mind, "Andrew, you didn't finish college, now did you?"

Mrs. Clarke reached out to her husband to make him stop, but he pulled away saying flippantly, "Hey, I'm just asking."

Knowing the circumstances of the day, I saw the immediate effect of betrayal, as the light in her eyes dimmed, and her body confidence wilted.

Just then one of the stewards came up to Mrs. Clarke and asked, "Do you have a fan somewhere? There are a lot of bees around the wine table."

Flustered, Mrs. Clarke said, "Yes, in the shed."

The steward questioned, "Where?"

And then Jack and Andrew both spoke up at the same time and said, "I'll get it."

But Mr. Clarke couldn't help himself and said with a smart mouth attitude, "Sure, the shed."

Mrs. Clarke put up her hand and said to her husband, "I'll get it." Then turned and started to walk down towards the shed. Uncle David was walking up and asked her, "What's going on?"

She replied, "I'm done".

He asked, "What happened?"

She said, "He aggravates me to no end."

He asked, "Can I help?"

She answered, "No, there's nothing you can do."

I watched as she continued to the shed and Uncle David walked up to us looking like he was going to give Mr. Clarke a piece of his mind. Mrs. Clarke opened the shed door and went in. I saw the door close and heard the snap it makes when it springs shut behind you. The orchestra was playing its first song and I could hear the words,

And so, it was, the later, as the miller told his tale,
that her face at first just ghostly,
turned a whiter shade of pale.

Mrs. Clarke had been in the shed for maybe ten or fifteen seconds, when the door swung open, and out she fell, backwards, flailing her arms in the air, and with the full force of the fall, her head hit the stone walkway, and then bounced up, limp, like a lifeless ragdoll.

I'm sure the horror could be seen in our eyes. Mr. Clarke heard everyone's screams, turned, saw her on the ground and ran to her. The medical team's action was swift. Just the immediate family was let close. We all stood back. This couldn't be happening. The music stopped, but that song kept playing over and over in my head. They tried, but they couldn't resuscitate, and she never gained consciousness.

What happened? Why? How? The report said, "Once inside the shed, she reached up, took the fan off an upper shelf, and put it on the counter. And then by evidence and the scuff mark on her shoe, she then kicked the bucket that was on the floor, the one with the bowling bag in it, and when she kicked it, it dislodged from a bee's nest that was attached to it from the back side. The bees swarmed instantly, Mrs. Clarke stepped back fighting them off, the heel of her shoe got caught in a hole in the rotted flooring, she lost her balance and fell backward out of the shed, hit her head on the stone walkway, and died instantly."

It was all a nightmare, and she was gone, done. The world mourned and history will tell the details of the days that followed and how those days dragged on in our hearts like anchors and buried us in a sea of despair, grief, and guilt. Two years passed and the sorrow was still smothering. I wished it was just a bad dream, but it wasn't.

Then suddenly, my phone went off, and I was shaken out of my memories and into real time. I was at my desk and it was Janie calling to let me know I was invited to the White House for her father's re-election. She said, they would send a car and asked me if I could stay the night. I said, of course, and then let my boss know.

THE CATALYST

Two days later, on Tuesday, November 2nd, 2032, Election Day, I packed my bag, the car showed up, and on the way, I closed my eyes and thought about Mrs. Clarke. Two years had passed since she died, and the pain stuck as if it were yesterday. When I arrived at the White House Janie met me at the door. We hugged and I told her, "You look great!"

She looked at me and said, "I'm exhausted."

I said, "No, you look great."

And then she smiled and looked just like her mother. We hugged again and she said, "Thank you so much for being here."

I told her, "I wouldn't want to be anywhere else."

We hugged more and she told me, "Jack isn't here yet, but is on his way, we've got a little time, so let's go to my room and catch up."

The house was quiet, as if there was a pall over it. I asked her who was coming. She told me, "Not very many. Of course, Mr. Hal is already here, but Miss Janine won't be. Hal Jr. is moving to another place and she's helping to get him settled in this week."

I asked her, "How's he doing?"

She said, "Mr. Hal doesn't say much, but this is his second place in about a year. They just can't seem to help break his depression. I heard him tell my father that a million dollars couldn't fix his son."

I said, "Wow, that's a tough one."

She nodded yes, and said, "Uncle David will be here, and that's about it. My grandparents, bless their hearts, are so old, and it's too much for them to come out for this."

I asked, "How are they doing?"

She said, "Hanging in there, still in their house, they've got help. We don't see them much," and paused, "nothing's been the same..." and she started to cry.

I put my arm around her, and she wept, "I miss my mother so much."

I had no words. With a few deep breaths and a little time, she gathered herself together and asked me, "Come on, tell me what you're up to. Are you loving being back in D.C. again?"

I started to tell her I was seeing that guy, Christopher, the poet, the one from Brooklyn, he'd moved to Washington, when there was a knock at her door letting us know that they were ready for us in the living room.

As we headed down the hallway we ran into Jack. We all hugged. He said he just got there and would be down soon. He hugged his sister again and held on to her a bit longer. She thanked him for coming and he said, “I’m here because you asked me. I’m your brother.”

He went onto his room and as we walked downstairs, I asked Janie, “How’s he doing?”

She said, “Better, except he won’t open up. Same as my father, got a problem, won’t talk about it.”

“How is your dad doing?”

She sighed, “He’s been sick. I think he’s sick tonight. Stomach, nothing agrees with him.”

“And what about you?”

She said, “Honestly, I hoped that he wouldn’t do another four years. I’m emotionally drained and doing this, over and over, every day, out in the public, I’m barely holding on.”

The starkness of her words did not contrast with the atmosphere in the living room. There stood Mr. Clarke and Mr. Hal with a drink in their hand and bags under their eyes. We hugged, and as I looked around, I was engulfed by an abundance of loss that encompassed the entire essence of the evening. Nothing much to say. Jack came in, threw his father a wave from across the room and stood off to the side and talked with Janie and me.

It was early, about five and we were to have dinner at six. Uncle David was on his way. It wasn't going to be a party, per se, low key, just dinner and Mr. Clarke was scheduled to go to a local hotel later to thank the people and give his acceptance speech.

Just then a Security Official came in and told Mr. Clarke that there was an attempted hijack of a plane heading for Washington. It was thwarted, they were already on the ground, those involved were being transferred here to the local office, and they would have more details in just a few minutes.

Then more Security came in and gave a briefing. Apparently, a man grabbed a woman when she came out of a lavatory, right behind the cockpit door. He put a knife to her throat, saying he had a bomb. Immediately, another woman sitting in an aisle seat in the first row, jumped up and somehow got the hijacker to release the first woman and have him take her as a hostage instead. People were screaming and when the first woman got back to her seat with her three children she yelled over the screams, what some people thought was "thank you" and then the hijacker just buckled, let the second woman go, fell to the floor, and then threw up. He didn't resist, was restrained by some passengers and crew, and taken into custody when they landed.

It was already all over the news when Uncle David arrived. He asked, "What's going on?"

We were telling him when my phone went off. It was Christopher, messaging me saying, "The woman on the plane is my aunt."

I let everyone know right away, "I know the woman on the plane, I've met her."

Mr. Hal asked, "Which one?"

I said, "It has to be the second one, because I know she doesn't have any children."

There were a lot of questions and I told them what I knew about her, which wasn't much. I couldn't remember anything she had specifically said when I met her in 2027. I drew a blank. Mr. Hal pressed me for more, "Did you see her as a threat or dangerous?"

I told him, "I only met her once and she was nice. Her nephew thinks the world of her, and so I would say friend, not foe and so the answer is no, no threat, no danger."

Mr. Hal swung his head back and said, "Well, that's nothing substantial to go by."

Then Security let us know that both hostages, the woman with the children, and Christopher's aunt were being held for more questioning just down the street along with all the baggage they brought with them on the plane.

In a short amount of time, it was confirmed that Christopher's aunt had intervened and seemed to be a saving grace. There still was more information to be digested and word was that the woman with the children was being released to her family, but Christopher's aunt was still being detained, as they had more questions, wasn't anything serious, but it was going to be awhile.

Janie asked, "How long?"

And they said, "Maybe a couple more hours? Could be less."

Surprisingly, Jack spoke up and asked, "Does she have to stay there in that holding area?"

Mr. Hal said, "Of course she's got to stay there, where else would she stay?"

Jack said, "Well, she could come here."

Mr. Hal dismissed Jack's notion by saying, "That's ridicules."

"Why?" asked Jack.

"Because there's no need."

Jack stammered, "No need? She saves a plane full of people, and you say no need?" And then he went on all emotional, "If my mother were here, you know what she'd say? Especially, in light of what we know, she'd insist that we bring her here, so we can thank her properly for what she's done."

Janie stood with her brother on this and implored her father to consider it. Uncle David gave his support. And after a lot of haranguing by Mr. Hal, that didn't seem to make any sense, Mr. Clarke reluctantly agreed that it would be okay to have her brought to the White House, but if there were questions to be asked, Mr. Hal would do the asking. In a short time, Christopher's aunt was escorted over.

When they brought her in, she looked smaller than I remembered. She shook hands with Mr. Clarke and acknowledged me with a nod and a smile. I asked her if she remembered me, and she said, "Oh yes," and smiled again saying, "my sister and I talk almost every day." I held her hand and thanked her.

Everyone was introduced and she was asked if they could get her anything. She said, "Wine, please, red if you have it." They brought out a small cheese and cracker plate with the wine, and she was grateful.

Mr. Hal gave her an obligatory "appreciation" speech for what she had done, and then proceeded to start his grilling, subtle, but grilling none-the-less. He let her know, that they had some questions about what happened, saying it was hard to believe that she just jumped up and did what she did, and they were hoping that she would walk them through the whole thing.

She said she would tell them everything they wanted to know and asked, "Where do you want me to start?"

At first, he said, "Let's start at the beginning." But then he threw suspicion into the mix, when he asked her, "Tell me about where you were sitting, we know that you didn't buy a first-class ticket? How did you get up there?"

She took a sip of wine and then another and said, "When I arrived at the airport, they told me it was a full flight and I'd have to get my seat assignment at the gate. The woman at the gate said they were working on it and weren't sure yet. I told her, didn't matter what seat, it's a short flight, and I'll take whatever they have. She smiled and thanked me. A short time later they called my name and she told me that they were putting me in first-class, saying that's how it all worked out, and I thanked her."

Mr. Hal questioned, "Really?"

She said, "Of course really, I'm sure you can check it out."

"So," he asked, "Tell me, did you meet with the hijacker or the other woman at any time before the flight?"

She said, "Why don't I tell you everything I saw, everything I did, and what I was thinking? Because I remember everything clearly and I can tell, no offense, with you asking questions like that, we could be here all night."

Mr. Hal looked offended and then grunted saying, “Go ahead.”

She went on, “I was waiting in the first-class boarding group. I saw the woman with the children, she was not only in first-class, but pre-boarding because of the children. Easy to see when you’re standing in line. I also saw the hijacker guy, just the back of his head. I remember thinking, Kenny Rogers hair, not the white-haired Kenny, but the younger, salt and pepper, Kenny. They both boarded ahead of me. My boarding pass said row one, seat C, pretty much the seat right behind the cockpit, and I thought, wow, this should be the seat for an Air Marshall, not for an older woman.”

“Why? Why would you think that?” asked Mr. Hal.

She answered, “Who wouldn’t? I was thinking they give more instructions to someone in an exit row.”

“So, you were thinking something was going to happen?”

"No, I'm just telling you what went through my mind." She paused and said, "Let me go on. During the flight, only the children of the woman came up to use the lavatory, which was directly in front of me, but off to the left. When they told us over the speaker that we had a half hour until landing, the mother of the children came up to use the lavatory. While she was in there, the guy with the Kenny Rogers hair came up and waited outside the lavatory door."

Mr. Hal asked, "What did you think when you saw him standing there?"

She said, "At first I thought, that's a heavy tweed coat he has on, and then I looked down at his shoes and I saw that not only were they derelict, but his pant legs were too long, and it looked like he had been walking on the backs of them for weeks, as they were ripped and caked with dirt."

Mr. Hal questioned again, "What did you think when you saw all of that?"

She said, "It reminded me of a man I saw in Montreal once."

"So, you think you know him?"

Exasperated she said, "No, that was over thirty years ago. I was in Montreal, a little bit of a trip to a church there, the one with all the crutches that were left from those who were healed, I can't remember the name, anyway, my mother's family is from there. It was winter and I was on a tour of the church and this guy, so similar with the Kenny Rogers hair and heavy overcoat, was in the group. The church is several stories high and when we were going up to the next floor, that guy was in front of me on the escalator, and I could see that he had dirty worn shoes and the cuffs of his pant legs were ripped and muddied."

And then Mr. Hal asked, "Well, isn't it a little odd that you remember a man's pants and shoes from so many years ago?"

She said, "Sure, but the real reason why I remember him was because later, after the tour, I took the escalator up to the outside Basilica on the upper most level of the church and found myself alone up there kneeling at the altar, when I heard something, looked over, and saw him hiding behind a statue. He started to come towards me and kept saying in a French accent, the F word. It was a long way to get to the top of the escalator and he kept coming and repeating the F word. I got to the escalator before he got to me, and that's why I remember him so well."

Mr. Hal said, "That's a strange story."

And she said, "Strange but true."

Beleaguered he said, "Go on."

She continued, "So this guy is standing outside the lavatory for only a few seconds when the woman comes out, he grabs her with his left arm, turns her towards the passengers and with his right hand puts a knife to her throat, and it was then that I knew I had to do something."

Mr. Hal pushed back, "Why? Why did you think you had to do something? What's the reason?"

She looked at him and said, "Well, I actually have two reasons."

Impatient, Mr. Hal almost screams, "You have two reasons?" And then acting like it is too much, slaps the palm of his hand on his forehead, and with vexation asks, "Can you be more specific?"

She takes a deep breath and says, "One reason was because of a horrifying image I remembered from the eighties. I had an old black and white television, a plane had been hijacked, one passenger was killed, and we watched as the body was thrown out of the plane and onto the tarmac, where it lay for hours. When I saw this guy put a knife to her throat, I just thought, it'll be me before it's her."

It was a stark gruesome picture she painted, and we were all impacted, but Mr. Hal mockingly pressed her as if it made no sense to him, "Oh so courageous, … I don't get it. Why you instead of her? And even if you thought all that stuff, how'd you think you'd pull it off? Do you know karate? Do you have superpowers we don't know about?"

She took a deep breath and another sip of wine, slowed it down, and said, "If you let me, I'll try to get to the whole story." Then she looked at all of us, smiled and said, "What I did wasn't a vacant-minded, knee-jerk reaction, but you should know, that I was sure, in a split second, that I would try to put myself in her place, and that's when I got up." And then turning her attention to Mr. Hal, she asked, "Now if you want all the specifics? I've got them, but we'll have to move it along." And then focusing directly on Mr. Clarke, she said, "Or you'll miss your acceptance speech."

Mr. Clarke gave Mr. Hal the signal to speed it up and he continued with his questioning, "Alright, so what's the other reason?"

She said, "When I was in my late forties, I was distraught about the choices I had made."

Mr. Hal moaned.

She begged him with a look, and went on, "Especially my choice to wait too long, until I was too old, to bear a child, to become a mother. I feared this image of a barren future and couldn't rid myself of regret. Then one night I had a vivid dream, and it scared me so much that I couldn't function. I felt like I was dying, and no one could help me."

"Alright, let's stop it there. Do we have to hear your dreams?" And then he went on sarcastically, "So you had a bad dream, let me guess, it was on a plane, right?"

Christopher's aunt stayed calm and said, "No, not on a plane." Then she had a bite of cheese and another sip of wine. She offered to give us a brief look into her dream and we all agreed we wanted to hear it, overriding Mr. Hal's, for no good reason, opposition.

She said, "In my dream I was driving in Boston on the road that runs along the Charles River, the

Hatch Shell is off to my left, and a 60's high rise apartment building, with a sign that says, *If you lived here, you'd be home now*, was off to my right. The road was only two lanes wide and there were Jersey barriers on each side, with no shoulder. The traffic was stopped way down at the light. My car and the car to my left were the last two stopped cars in this long line of traffic, when behind us comes a semi-truck that can't seem to stop. I brace for the impact and then my dream fast-forwards to the accident scene. Clearly someone had been killed, and the truck driver was talking to the police officer saying, 'I couldn't stop and had to decide what to do, at the last second I saw a *Baby on Board* sign and so I hit the other car.' It was then I realized that it was me and I was dead."

Even Mr. Hal was stunned a bit into silence, and I think, by that time, we all had our mouths open.

She continued, "It was so real. I woke up knowing I was dead. Dead because I had squandered my chances and never became the mother I wanted to be, and for that, not only could I not forgive myself, but I found myself drowning in the darkness and depths of that dreaded dream and my doomsday death. I couldn't function, fear had a grip on me. Somehow, I clung to a small flicker of light I had seen once when I was a child, and with my fingernails crawled out of the fateful hole I had dug. Over time, I finally came to think differently about the dream. I thought about the mother in the other car. Was her child in the car with her? I couldn't see. I thought of her family, after the accident, and their elation to hear she was alright. Then I thought, what if it was my daughter in that car? Would I have given my life for her and for my grandchild? Would I have begged the truck driver to hit me, to take me, to let me die instead of them? In a moment of inspiration, in my heart I became a mother, courageous, willing to die for my child. I was thankful and my fear was lifted. It was then I vowed, promised, if I was ever in a situation, like I was today on the plane, with a mother's life on the line, that I would gladly take her place, without hesitation, as if she were my own."

We were reeling in our seats. The dynamics of her story, the dimension of the dream, and the cadence of her voice, made me feel like I was going in and out of a window.

Mr. Hal couldn't control himself and had to say something stupid, "Sounds like a death wish to me."

You could hear the groans coming from all of us, pleading with Mr. Hal to stop being such a jerk.

She asked for another inch of wine and said to Mr. Hal, "I really hope this helps answer any questions about why I did what I did?"

I think we all kind of nodded yes, and I don't think we even knew where we were in the story anymore. Not as impressed, Mr. Hal took control and suggested we get back to the timeline of what happened.

Christopher's aunt went on, "Like I said, once I saw the knife at her throat, I got up out of my seat, I looked directly at him, and then took my left hand and put it on his right hand the one that was holding was holding the knife, and I said, something like, 'let her go to her kids, take me instead,' and then he loosely lightened the knife on her throat, and I said to her, 'go to your children.' I kept my hand on his hand and he released just enough for her to squirm down and as she did, I turned the right side of my body into the hold that he had on her, and at the same time, I took my hand off his hand, and he put the knife right to my throat.

"People were screaming, and the woman scurried down the aisle back to her children and once there, turned. I can see her, she looks right at us, but speaks directly to the hijacker, and says loudly, so everyone will hear, 'Thank you. Thank you.' I don't think it took more than a second, and he started to go limp, buckling, letting go of the grip on the knife, and falling to the floor. I moved away as he started to vomit, and people pounced on him to make sure he was down."

By then we were all taking a gulp of wine when Mr. Hal asked, "What time is it?" We were lost in the intrigue. I almost forgot she was Christopher's aunt or where I was.

The Security Team came in to update Mr. Clarke, "We're sure the hijacker acted on his own and none of the parties knew each other. He did have a bomb and could have detonated it. When we asked the woman with the children, why she thanked him, she said it was because he let her go, when she knew he didn't have to. She went on to say that even though she knew there was still a possibility that they might all die, she remembered what she promised when the knife was at her throat, 'if she could just get back to her children, she would be grateful,' and that's why she thanked him.

"As far as the hijacker, he's had severe issues and depression for years, somewhat homeless, saved all his money for this first-class flight, and seemed bound and determined to take the plane down. He couldn't account in his mind why he eased up on the knife or why he let the first woman go, but he does remember the look in the woman's eyes when she said 'thank you' to him. He said he had never been thanked before, not really thanked for anything. He said her words lifted him almost immediately, and for the first time in his life, he felt something, a connection, a caring for this woman, and in that caring realized he didn't want to kill her or anyone else, and that's why he fell to the floor and gave up."

Then one of the Security Officers took Mr. Hal aside to show him something, and when he came back in, Mr. Hal said to Christopher's aunt, "They had to go through all of your bags, and they found this."

He held up an old yellowed, dirt-stained, use to be white, piece of paper. When opened, it was letter size, it had deep visible creases from years of being folded and on the corners where the folds were, there were small holes that looked like four-pointed stars with a long tail, except for the fact that it had typed words on it, it reminded me of the Shroud of Turin.

She looked at him and said, “Yes?”

He started reading, “If I was ever harmed, intentionally or unintentionally, and I couldn’t speak for myself, that I would want everyone to know, if I had any say, that I would forgive the person, no matter what, no penalty, no punishment.” He stopped reading and sternly asked, “What’s all this nonsense about forgiving everyone no matter what they do? What kind of world do you think we live in? And why did you take it on the plane with you?”

It was getting late, dinner was put on hold, she looked tired and said to us, “First of all, if you want to know, I’ll try to be brief.”

Our interest was aroused once again, and we wanted to hear what she had to say, and Mr. Hal gave a reluctant go ahead.

"First of all, I always carry it with me. I had it drawn up by an attorney over thirty years ago, and if something ever happens to me, I want people to know that I'm a total forgiver."

Mr. Hal goes off wild, "So someone can just come in and kill you, beat you, and you'll be fine with it? Let him go, no problem. That's craziness! How about the rest of us, you going to forgive them for killing us too? How does that work?"

She answered, "I don't know how it all works, but I'm saying, for me, just for me, that I am willing, up front, to forgive in advance, whatever might or could happen to me in the future."

"That's the most insane notion I've ever heard!" cried Mr. Hal. "How the heck do you think we'd all survive if everyone thought your way?" Shaking uncontrollably, he looked at us, pointed his finger toward his head and made a circling motion as if she was crazy and said, "I could tell right away, there was something up with her."

Our eyes were blurry, and our senses had been rattled, we all tried to jump to her defense with words or motions, but she insisted with a smile, it wasn't necessary.

Security came in and told Mr. Clarke that Christopher's aunt's husband was waiting for her and they were ready to let her leave. Mr. Hal looked over at Mr. Clarke, shrugged his shoulders and said, "I guess I'm done."

Uncle David and us three kids thanked her again, for everything. There were hugs all around and she left. Mr. Hal was grumbling over what just happened and Mr. Clarke didn't look too good.

Everything I wanted to say about that night, I couldn't, not right away. It was mind blowing. My head was spinning from the stories she told and the reality of the evening. Against my boss's wishes, I needed some quiet time, so while others went on to the acceptance speech, I went to my room early.

THE AFTERMATH

The next morning, I got up late, and met Janie and Jack in the breakfast room. They were talking about the hijacking affair and the bad nightmare Mr. Clarke had. I told them I was out like a light and didn't hear a thing. Janie said, "He hasn't had one in two years, but maybe it's because he's been sick lately."

"Lately?" cried Jack. "He's been sick for years. Did you see him last night? He just sat there with that vacant look in his eyes. Not a word."

"It's because he's not feeling well." defended Janie.

"No, it's because he's sick, sick in the head. Sick with how he treats our grandparents, with Andrew, and I'm sorry, but look what he did to Mom."

Janie gasped, "No."

"Yes, he pushed her to the brink, we all know it. Mister too proud, more important than anyone else."

"Please Jack," she pleaded, "it's too much." And she started to cry.

Their pain was palpable. They hugged and said they loved each other. Jack said he was sorry, but he had to leave. He said he would have stayed for her sake but was afraid that things might blow up between him and his father. "I have no respect for him."

Again, she cried, "Jack."

He replied, "Dad's got you here and look at you, wasting your life for someone who hasn't even cried, has he? Has he cried for Mom, for us, for anybody? He's empty! He's a sorry sort of a man. It's all about him. He doesn't feel well. He doesn't want to talk about it. As far as I'm concerned, he's an emotional no show. He's ruined everything."

The raw truth was difficult, and Janie wept openly.

I left them alone and went to check my messages, as my boss was calling nonstop. The hijack story hit the news and was growing by the minute. I had planned to leave the White House mid-morning. Janie had her own "First Family" duties that day and was filling in for her father because he was too sick to leave his bed. As we hugged goodbye, it was scary how sad she appeared, and how forlorn she seemed, like her mother on her last day.

In the next two weeks there were thousands upon thousands of stories surrounding the hijacking and those involved. The story fascinated people. So many avenues to expand upon. Christopher's aunt, the mother with the children, and the hijacker all had their real lives dredged up, re-concocted and spun like tops; and like wildfire, the image of courage and the essence of gratitude, spread around the globe, along with scepticism and tightened security.

Of course, when it came to Christopher's aunt, her stories took on a life of their own. People who knew her came out of the woodwork, many to say they had heard her tell some of those stories before. Even the lawyer who drew up the now famous or infamous *forgiveness statement* was still alive and remembers Christopher's aunt well and with fondness. Copies of the *forgiveness statement* quickly circulated around the world and almost immediately, for so many reasons, people supplanted their name, held it on their person, and embraced it as their own.

From a practical standpoint, this whole notion about *total forgiveness* was lamb-basted as a fairy tale and most of the discussion discounted Christopher's aunt as an old, out of touch, left over, from the sixties.

The White House had to take a stand. Mr. Hal was sure to let everyone know that they consider it, "Nonsense, just nonsense." And then speaking about Christopher's aunt, he said, "Nice woman, don't get me wrong, but the whole idea of *blanket forgiveness* is complete nonsense."

About three weeks had passed, and it was the day before Thanksgiving. Janie and I had planned to get together early, meet some old friends, and she asked me to spend the night at the White House and stay for Thanksgiving Brunch. We saw Mr. Clarke as he was heading out to a Presidential Breakfast in Northern Virginia and afterwards, he was going to make a short stop to see his parents. They asked him to come by, as they couldn't make it to the White House for Thanksgiving. Mr. Clarke looked annoyed as if he didn't want to visit them, but plans were set and off he went.

I said to Janie, "The last time I was here, he wasn't doing too good?"

She said she didn't want to talk about it too much, as it made her depressed, "But his nightmares are back with a vengeance and his stomach problems are wreaking havoc with his system."

In the early evening Uncle David arrived. He was spending the night too, so he could have Thanksgiving Brunch with us. It was unusual for Mr. Hal not to be there, but supposedly Miss Janine gave him some kind of ultimatum and so they were spending Thanksgiving with Hal Jr. Jack called at the last minute and said he couldn't make it and promised Janie he would see her soon.

When Mr. Clarke returned from the visit with his parents, he was agitated, barely said a word, and headed to the den for a drink. Uncle David, Janie, and I followed him in. He started talking as if only Uncle David was in the room. "They called me in and told me that they were old, and they would like to have some closure. My father asked me point blank, 'What have I done wrong? Why don't you love me?' I could only see my brother's face, and I could feel my blood curdle."

Uncle David asked, "Well maybe this is what you've needed, did you tell him why?"

"Yes, I was so angry at first, but I finally found the words and told him what I saw that last night before my brother left for Vietnam. What I heard my brother say, that he 'was scared,' and what I heard my father tell him, 'there's no yellow in this family.' I poured my heart out and told him how it's festered inside me all these years."

"What did he say?" asked Uncle David.

The veins in Mr. Clarke's neck looked like they were going to explode, and as he reached for words, he started to tremble and screamed, "He said, it never happened. Just like that, denied that it ever happened. I wanted to choke him."

"Really? Did he say anything else?"

"Yeah, he said he remembered every minute of every day of that last week my brother was home. He said he remembered every time he looked at him, every touch of his hand, every kiss on his forehead, every second, every last second, he had with him. He said he loved him, as if he were his own, and that he never said or would have ever said anything like what I claimed to have seen and heard that last night. According to him, it simply didn't happen and then he and my mother hugged me and said they wished we had talked about this years ago."

"Wow!" said Uncle David. "What do you make of that?"

"What do I make of that?" growing louder, his face getting redder, "I think he's an old man that conveniently forgets what he wants to forget. I spent my whole life reliving that night and what he did, and he just blows it off, gives me a hug, and thinks it will all go away."

It was a traumatic evening and later that night, after Mr. Clarke and Janie went to bed, Uncle David and I stayed up and talked. We backtracked over the story about what Mr. Clarke had seen and heard as a young boy and how it still laid over him like a plague, suffocating his spirit and stifling his reason.

Over the next few days Janie kept me in the loop. She said her father had become mad at the world. She was nervous because there was a planned "First Family" activity coming up in mid-December. She told me, "There's going to be a public formal ceremony at the Vietnam Veteran's Memorial. My grandparents are going to be there, and Jack says he's coming. My father is supposed to place a wreath near his brother's name." And as she went on, I was surprised to hear that Mr. Clarke had never been to the Wall.

A few days later I got a call from Andrew, who said he was going to be in Washington and wanted to take me to lunch and we agreed to meet. He and I hadn't talked much over the last few years and it was good catching up. The talk went to the last time we were together, the day Mrs. Clarke died, and without saying much, we cried. He said, "A day doesn't go by without her running through my mind, making me smile. I miss her and I miss him too."

I asked, "Really? Even with that whole thing, him cutting you out, like he did?"

"I got over it," and then said so easily, "I let it go and just remembered the good parts. Because of them I had a super childhood. I was able to me, Andrew, and in the end, I liked me. But I have to say that without Mrs. Clarke, I might not have ever caught onto the bigger things. When I think of her, I breath, I slow down, and watch where I'm going, and when everyone around me calls gloom, I remember her laughing, finding the good." He smiled, touched my hand, and said, "Make sure you let everyone know that I'm grateful for everything."

The rest of the meeting with Andrew was awash with fun memories and when we parted, for the first time, in over ten years, it was clear to me how Andrew was doing, and it was good.

On the morning of the Vietnam Memorial Service Jack and I arrived at the White House. Mr. Clarke's parents would go directly to the Wall. Jack, Janie, and I went in one car and Mr. Clarke went in another. On the way Janie said, "He's still out of his mind about this whole thing with his father. I'm hoping we get through this day without him getting sick."

Jack just gazed out the car window and said, "I have no use for him."

It was a cold and drizzling day. The place was packed for the event and news cameras were everywhere. Mr. Clarke's father was in a wheelchair and his mother steadied herself with the help of an assistant. The ceremony was brief, and a wreath was placed next to where his brother's name was engraved.

Mr. Clarke was asked if he wanted to make a rubbing and he said no, and then they encouraged him to at least touch his brother's name, and he reluctantly agreed.

I was close enough to see just a part of his hand, not his fingers, as he touched the Wall, and ran them over his brother's name. Suddenly, he threw his head back and I thought he was about to sneeze, but then I saw that he was almost convulsing. His arm was stretched out and his fingers seemed glued to the Wall, and like a man whose life passes before his eyes, his body pulsed, as if being electrically charged. Everyone took notice. When he finally broke away, he turned, fell to his knees, and crawled just the few steps over to his father's lap, clung to his legs, looked up at him and cried out loud, "Oh my God, it wasn't you, it was me! He was talking to me! Oh my God, what have I done! All this time, it was me!"

Immediately, the Secret Service swarmed around, sheltered them, and whisked them away. It caused quite a stir and was covered extensively by the press. Everyone wanted to know what was going on. Was he alright? What did it all mean?

Back at the White House he was inconsolable and only wanted to see Uncle David and told him that when he touched his brother's name on the Wall, he was shocked into seeing, into knowing, into fully realizing that he had been wrong all those years, his whole life, that it wasn't his father his brother came to talk to that night, it was him, and he was the one who told his brother, 'there's no yellow in this family.'

All night he screamed he wanted to die. Sometimes he would wail and other times he would just scream the word no. He wouldn't leave his room. Word was he stayed in a fetal position, sometimes on the bed and sometimes on the floor.

When the public asked about the incident at the Wall, Mr. Hal made the excuse that Mr. Clarke was, "Just coming to terms with his brother's death and subsequently his wife's death." It was plausible and the people and press gave him a little room to grieve.

Two days went by, Mr. Clarke did not improve. Mr. Hal said openly, "I just don't understand why something like that would throw a man over the edge."

Uncle David had a completely different take on it. He saw what Mr. Clarke saw, the whole horrifying realization that his unwillingness to confront the agitation from within and clear the air early on, resulted in heartbreak and tragedy for his entire family. "He says he just wants to die, that he doesn't deserve to live, and he can never be forgiven." Janie cried and Jack held her.

Mr. Hal thought he should be the one to try and make him see reality. "I know him, he'll listen to me and he'll shake this thing off." And then said, "If he's not better by tomorrow, I'm going in." Tomorrow came, nothing was better, and Mr. Hal went in.

We could hear it from the hallway, before Mr. Hal could even get a word out. Mr. Clarke screamed at him, "Get out! Leave me alone. I don't care, you got it! Let somebody else do it, I'm finished!" Mr. Hal tried to persist but was forcibly screamed out of the room.

Mr. Clarke's doctor was concerned and said, if Mr. Clarke keeps taking some fluids, he would give us another couple of days before he had to do more.

I called my boss and told him I needed to stay at the White House for a while, even though he knew I couldn't say why, he told me no problem, take all the time you need. He said there were stacks of articles about Christopher's aunt for me to follow up on and said he would send them to me, maybe I'd find some time to look them over. There were thousands and thousands of stories from around the world, all of them about how people were climbing out of personal darkness, despair, and depression, by using Christopher's aunt's *forgiveness statement* as a ladder, a bridge, or a safe haven. They were inspirational and I shared some of them at the White House. Mr. Hal was still sticking to the whole nonsense thing, and Uncle David had been grappling with his faith, but found something about it promising, far-fetched, but promising... However, Jack and Janie were showing signs of defeat. Because their father hadn't, they hadn't properly mourned their mother's death, and now with him spiralling out of control, their world was caving in and everything about their life seemed for not.

Time was clicking down and Mr. Clarke teetered on a desperate edge. In just over a week, he had gone from robust, inflated, and red-faced, to feeble, sunken-eyed, and almost unrecognizable. Sometimes he was lucid enough to say that he was sure he could never recover from what he had done. "Recovery," he cried, "It only means I live longer and so does the pain, the guilt, and the shame." When Janie begged him to try, he stroked her hair and with his fingers wiped away her tears, shook his head no, and moaned, "I'm sorry, I can't."

I knew I shouldn't have, but I called my mother and told her what was going on, only because I knew she wouldn't say anything. After listening, she said she wasn't shocked to hear that about Mr. Clarke. She tried to take my mind off it and asked if things were still good with Christopher, and I told her yes. And without me mentioning them, she then went on about the stories she was reading about Christopher's aunt and the personal phenomena people were experiencing after embracing the now known *forgiveness statement* and then questioned me, "Have you thought about asking her, maybe she can help?"

It was a long shot, but maybe Christopher's aunt could help and so I suggested it. Of course, Mr. Hal railed about the absurdity, and didn't see how she could. Uncle David said it couldn't hurt, but he was tired of trying to help someone who wouldn't help himself, leaving it up to Jack and Janie. Janie said, "If she'll come, yes, please, anything."

Jack, still resistant, while holding his sister in his arms responded, "Whatever she wants."

I called Christopher's aunt on Wednesday, December 22nd, explained the backstory of Mr. Clarke's plight, she agreed to come on Friday the 24th, and said it was good timing, as on that day she and her husband were leaving on a train out of Washington for a six-week vacation and she could come by for about an hour around three. I remember thinking, is that going to be enough time? At the request of the White House, she agreed to keep the meeting hush hush.

Janie told her father they had asked Christopher's aunt to come by. Refusing to agree, he was reticent and did not want to discuss. It was scary to see the turn he had taken. He hadn't left his bed in days. His downturned face reflected the horror he kept behind his eyes, continuing to reference in his rambling, the images, and the reminders, that he was damaged, broken, and deservedly almost dead. With every passing hour, as he languished on the hinterland of some dangerously slippery slope, he became more and more enmeshed in a hapless, hopeless, and unhealthy hole. As he shook his head no, Janie cried and begged him to try harder, "Please for my sake." Desperate to save her father, she stood some ground, and after refusing to take "no" for an answer, he reluctantly agreed to the meeting with Christopher's aunt, saying he didn't think anything could help.

Plans were made and for the next day and a half, as we waited for her arrival, I had this pit in my stomach, thinking what the heck are we doing? And what could she possibly do or say to help him? The word surreal didn't begin to describe how thick the air was or how ominous impending uncertainty can sound.

Jittery, most of us tried to put on an optimistic face. Her visit became our "pie-in-the-sky" chance for Mr. Clarke, and we all hoped for the best, except for Mr. Hal, who threw scepticism around, as if he just couldn't shut his mouth.

THE VISIT

She was late, real late, so much so, that it was apparent she barely had five minutes before she would have to turn around and leave, ten if she stretched it. Uncle David was antsy, as he had obligations at his church, it being Christmas Eve and all. Mr. Hal was strutting around, like he was right all along, that this was a bad idea. Jack was out of it emotionally and stood with Janie, but only as a matter of brotherly support, and I was nervous, having set the whole thing up.

When she arrived, Mr. Hal denigratingly asked her with finger quotes, "Are you here to save the day?"

She smiled, clasped her hands together, brought them up under her chin, and with a little bit of a pointed finger said to him, "If I had to pick, I'd say that you'll be the first," and then pointing to us, "out of the five of you, to catch a glimpse of something going on."

He shook his head and said mockingly, "We're wasting our time here folks."

She noddingly agreed and on the way to Mr. Clarke's room I apologized for putting her on the spot, especially now, having almost no time. She graciously assured me it was fine, saying, "Sometimes less is more."

The meeting between Mr. Clarke and Christopher's aunt was being recorded, and if we wanted to, we could watch it live, as it happened, from the monitoring room, but Uncle David had to leave, Mr. Hal flat out refused, and Janie and Jack just couldn't, not right now, so I did.

When she entered, he was in bed, under the covers and looking gray. He hadn't shaved and despite somebody's attempt to keep his hair lying flat, it was sticking up like a spikey-toothed saw blade.

He was the first to speak and asked in a low voice, "Why are you here?"

She said, "To open a door, shine a light, clear the air."

He said, "I am not amused."

She answered, "As well you shouldn't be. I'm here because if you remain the same, the devastation caused by your lack of compassion will go down in history as monumental."

"What the heck are you talking about?"

Mincing no words, she said, "By your own admission, when your brother came to your room in the middle of the night, you clearly didn't show him compassion. You let him slump back to his room, broken, and then you watched him walk away the next morning, without a sorry being said."

He rose up a bit in his bed and shouted defiantly, "I was just seven, how dare you? I loved my brother!"

"But you didn't say what another seven-year-old might have said under the same circumstances, like, get under my bed, I'll hide you, I won't let them take you, or let me tell Dad, he'll know what to do."

"I was just a kid!"

"A kid without compassion, and then to make matters worse, you blamed your father for what you had done, and because you wouldn't talk about it, you fostered a grudge, you withheld affection from your parents, and ultimately ruined any loving relationship they could have hoped for with you, effectively leaving them with the loss of two sons."

Now weeping, he asks, "Why are you saying all of this?"

"Because it doesn't end there. Over the years, your loving wife, begged you, and begged you to open up about your nightmares, about the hostility you held for your father, and what it was doing to everyone, but you disregarded her pleas and denied you were causing any pain. You stifled her voice with the self-importance of your position and minimized her input and from what I've learned, she was suffering from an aggravation you caused on the day she died, something some say wouldn't have happened, if you had just been nicer."

Now he was whimpering, "No, no."

"Those awful memories are from your past, but you continue the same here in the present. I'll bet when your daughter asked you to meet with me, you made her beg for a long time and you let her cry before you agreed, and you probably told her you didn't think it would do any good anyways. I'll bet you know how much pain she's in right now, but you just can't seem to put her feelings before your own."

Now with tears streaming down his face he cries, “Don’t you think I know all this?”

“Well, just knowing it isn’t enough. If you are to live, you need to change. It’s Christmas Eve. Old Scrooge didn’t want to see what he had done, what he had become. It took three dreams to shake him to his core, to make him cry out loud and finally ask, is it too late to change?” She stopped talking and took a sip of water. “Look at you, dying like this. It’s a crying shame, your parents will go to their grave shattered and sadness will smother your children.” Taking a deep swallow, she continues, “You’re in a deadly predictable cycle, that’s why they called me here, I’ve been where you are, thinking I could never forgive myself for what I had done, but you’re wrong, just like all those years you thought you were right, you’re wrong.”

By then he was pulling up the blanket to cover his face.

She said, "You've been pulling the covers over your head your whole life and now you're dying in this dead-end darkness caused by your dishonest despair."

Moaning he cries, "Leave me alone, just leave me alone."

Persistent she goes on, "Have you ever had a good dream? Do you ever think of somebody other than yourself? Do you even know what that means?"

Now sobbing he mumbles, "Just let me die."

Firmly she comes back quick, "Mr. President, if you have marked yourself to die, then depart. You know the drill. Your casket will be made, the ground broken for your grave, and your children, well your children will be lost."

Shaking his head and sobbing he cries, "I can't, I wish I could, but I can't!"

And with a stone cold look on her face she replied, "There's an old western movie where a young boy faced with a difficult task pleads to his father, *I can't*, but his father, knowing better, turns to his son and says, *sometimes when you can't, you must*." She then forced a silence into the room and said no more.

He cried some more, slowly gathered himself, and then while exhaling and shaking through the tears he asked, "What if I don't want to die?"

She slowed it down, spoke softly but surely, and said, "I would smile, call you brother, and tell stories to rouse you from the fence, and make you be like a leader. Stories, when internalized, will help you better absorb, in the air, the value of the seeming intangible, from places where vibrant life forms, such as forgiveness and compassion are complete, and where vengeance isn't even a word. Then, and only then, should you choose to live, know this beyond a doubt, when forgiven, your soul will be charged by the light of the world and your heart will be called upon to loosen the stranglehold of judgement."

His eyes spun and he looked at her as if she had two heads and muttered, "What?"

She said, "The impulse will be so strong and the changes before you so great, that you will move forward, even without knowing where to put your feet."

He rolled his hands together in a ball, brought them up to his mouth, and in a confused, but sincere tone, said, "Wow, I don't even know what to make of that."

Smiling she said, "I think you will, not today, but soon. From what I can see, it's already started." Then looking at the time, she said, "I better go." He started to get up, but she told him not to, then walked over to his bedside, and like an older sister, kissed him on the forehead and said, "It's the time of year when angels appear and I'm your first." She laughed and then asked him, "Do me a favor, would you? Look for your brother to visit you, your wife too, it'll do you and them a world of good."

And out Mr. Clarke's bedroom door she went and was met in the hall by Mr. Hal who questioned her rudely, "Now, you wouldn't be the kind of person to go out and tell everyone that you had this silly meeting here today, would you?"

She smiled, touched him on the arm and said, "No, you will."

Annoyed by her answer, he walked away, murmuring something I didn't catch, grabbed his briefcase, and without saying Merry Christmas to anyone, left for home.

I was spending the night at the White House. It was a solemn night, Mr. Clarke did not come out of his room, but Janie and I took to the couch with our snacks and blankets to watch an old made-for-tv Christmas movie that she said her mother loved. Jack was going to be upstairs but kept coming through the living room for one reason or another and then sat on the arm of the couch to watch the end of the movie. He pointed to the screen and asked Janie with a grin, "Isn't that the guy mom used to call Doogie because she couldn't remember his real name?"

Janie smiled, the first one I'd seen from her in some time, and said, "Yes, it's him, she was so funny that way." Jack smiled and then tussled her hair. She tried to tussle his and they laughed together.

Jack said, "I love you kid."

She said, "Oh Jack, I love you too." And they hugged. I thought to myself, if nothing else on Christmas Eve, at least they have this.

But soon our attention was nicely turned to the ending of the movie and the final words from the grandfather's diary. I had never seen the movie and Janie said she couldn't remember the ending, so when the grandson read his grandfather's last words, "forgiveness is the most important thing," we were wowed with the relevance, as it echoed in each of us like soft thunder. It was a tearjerker, we were speechless, and left wiping our eyes.

The next morning, Janie and I had coffee. I was leaving the White House early, to meet with Christopher and my parents for Christmas Brunch. She said her father still hadn't come out of his room and sighed, and then asked me what Christopher's aunt said during the visit yesterday. I told her it was, "Somber, clairvoyant, almost cryptic."

She asked, "Is it something I want to see?"

I told her, "Some parts of it are painful." So, she decided against watching it, at least for the time being, and I agreed with her. But for me, no matter what I was doing, that visit kept running through my mind, like a strange fortune from a cookie.

ALL BETTER

The week between Christmas and New Year's Eve I was up to my ears with work. Christopher was going to Maine to spend time with his parents and invited me, but I couldn't leave. My boss had given all the stories about Christopher's aunt and this *forgiveness thing* to me. I was overwhelmed with the number, too numerous for me to count, and I wasn't sure which direction to go in. In retrospect, I was exhausted. The last two weeks at the White House did me in. I tried to read or reason but couldn't. I spoke with Janie and she told me her father had come out of his room and told both her and Jack that he was going to be better, but then didn't say much more than that. She said he watched the video of the visit with Christopher's aunt many times and then, against Mr. Hal's input, decided to go forward with a pre-scheduled New Year's Eve live interview, from the West Wing.

On New Year's Eve there was a heck of a snowstorm brewing when I arrived at the White House. Janie and I were heading to a private party after Mr. Clarke's interview which was going to be at eight o'clock. Jack wasn't sure he was going to go out but said maybe he'd tag along with us. Mr. Hal was there to coach Mr. Clarke through the interview and Miss Janine was with him. Hal Jr. was on his way. It was his birthday and the three of them were going out to dinner after the interview.

Mr. Clarke had agreed to the interview because an old friend in the media was going to be asking the questions, however, with the bad weather, his friend couldn't make it and so somebody else was being sent to conduct the interview. Mr. Hal was walking around like a pressure cooker, every "what if?" came to mind and he resorted to mumbling. Mr. Clarke, although shaky himself, suggested he calm down. Mr. Hal said, "It wouldn't be so bad, but then I've got to spend the night with my son, who I haven't seen since Thanksgiving, and it wasn't good then. It just gets worse, there's nothing to say."

Just before the interview started Janie and I were standing behind Mr. Clarke, and Mr. Hal and Miss Janine were standing directly across from us, facing Mr. Clarke. This was so Mr. Hal could see Mr. Clarke's face and give him signals if necessary. Jack was off to the side. They were setting the lights and I could see Mr. Clarke still looked haggard, not much better than what he looked a week ago. Then from behind us, in comes Hal Jr. I hadn't seen him since Mrs. Clarke's funeral, but something was very different. He seemed brighter. He was smiling and touched my arm and said hello. I smiled back, was going to say something, but the interview was just getting underway, and we had to be quiet.

The usual questions were asked, the economy, the fight against the unforeseen, but then the interviewer asked about Mr. Clarke's bad time at the Wall a couple of weeks ago, and I could see Mr. Hal trying to get Mr. Clarke's attention to try and avoid the question. But Mr. Clarke said, "I was reckoning with brother's death and things that happened years ago and it broke me to my knees."

Then the interviewer mentioned Christopher's aunt by saying, "That woman has started a lot of problems."

Mr. Clarke responded, "Why would you say that?"

"Well, you know she's pushing people to break the system, to forgive everything, everybody. It's turned into some kind of mini-cult."

"I don't think she's pushing anything."

"Well, there are some who think her view is causing quite a public menace."

"You've got to be kidding me?"

"No, I'm not and those who oppose her little paper on *total forgiveness* say she goes against every bit of the American grain and there should be some law against it."

Mr. Clarke replied strongly, "Last I knew, we all had the right to forgive anyone we wanted. That's our right, I mean we can't legislate against that. If I want to forgive someone, that's my right."

"But Mr. President, our country demands justice, and you must uphold ..."

Mr. Hal swiped his hand across his throat to signal the end and called the interviewer away from the table. Mr. Clarke got up abruptly, turned and walked toward us. He saw Hal Jr. and even though agitated, he forced a smile and said, "Hey Henry, Happy Birthday."

Hal Jr. smiled and stretched out his hand, Mr. Clarke shook it, looked Hal Jr. in the face and asked with an astonished tone, "What's happened? You've changed."

"Yes sir I have."

"It's significant."

"Yes sir, it is."

But before he could say anymore, Miss Janine called out to her son from the other side of the room. Hal Jr. turned to Mr. Clarke and said, "My parents don't know yet, let me tell them first." And then went across the room to see his parents.

With jaw dropped, Mr. Clarke turned to Janie and me and asked, "Did you see him?" We both said yes. A change was evident. His complete persona seemed stunningly spectacular, sensible, in charge. I watched him as he approached his parents. It didn't take more than a couple of seconds before both were grabbing at him and hugging him, pulling him close. There were gasps and cries of happiness coming from all three of them.

With weak knees Mr. Hal comes over to us. His eyes filled with tears, he grabs Mr. Clarke by the jacket lapels and almost crumbles to the floor. Mr. Clarke uses both arms to hold him up and all the while Mr. Hal is crying, "I got my son!" And then forcing Mr. Clarke to look him in the eye says, "Tell me did you see him? There's something going on, there's something going on."

Just then Uncle David arrives late. He sees that Mr. Hal is in a state and asks him, "Are you alright?"

Mr. Hal stumbles over, hugs him and cries, "There's something going on. It's my son. You need to see him."

Hal Jr. walks over to us with Miss Janine holding onto him. Uncle David takes one look and sees the undeniable demeanor transformation. At the same time Jack comes over and meets eyes with Hal Jr. and they have a ricochet connection and Jack says, "Wow dude, you're on fire."

This all happens within a couple of minutes. We were all supposed to be on our different ways for the New Year's festivities, but we all were so taken by the change we saw in Hal Jr. that we wanted to hear what happened, if he wanted to say. Right away Uncle David, citing the weather, suggested we all stay at the White House. Jack said we could order some food in. Janie asked her Dad and he said okay. Hal Jr. asked his parents if the change in plans would be alright and they both agreed, and soon we convened in the family living quarters around a table that fit all eight of us. Miss Janine made oolong tea.

An air of holiday and a rush that prompts heightened spirits to fill a room overtook us and like children waiting for family movie night, our expressions resonated with anticipation and excitement. The food arrived quickly, and we sat down together. Miss Janine wanted to say grace and cried tears of gratitude all the way through. Mr. Hal glowed with complete humility. A look I had never seen on him.

Uncle David spoke first, "Would you tell us what happened?"

Hal Jr. replied, "You all know me. Up until now, you've never heard me string more than four words together. I was meek. I couldn't meet eyes, I was a lost soul, out of the margin of touch, judged on the spectrum, alone inside, and severely depressed. I lived in fear, of some unspeakable fear. It was violent and I had no defense."

Miss Janine whimpered, "Oh no."

Hal Jr. put his arm around her and said, "It's alright Mom. That's over now." And he went on, "Then came the hijacking and I read everything about everyone involved. Although I was non-functioning on so many levels, I had a broad intellect with an ability to gather information and program the results. Numbers, statistics, rhythms, and patterns have always come easy to me; and so, I followed the stories of those who had revelations while grabbing onto this thing called *total forgiveness*, and how for those who forgave up front, before the fact and without question, had their lives dramatically changed."

He took a sip of tea and went on, "They were old and young, rich and poor, the afflicted and the addicted, victims and victimizers, aggressors and passives, the delusional and deranged, the homeless and those who have never had a bed. They came from all over the world and from as varied situations that one could imagine. Every story culminated with a promise to forgive, no matter what. To say yes to the end of human-on-human brutality, no matter what. The cheek to be turned, ahead of time, effecting the end of judgement, one person at a time."

He was so intense and continued, "In just a couple of weeks and because of my connections," pointing to his father, "I was fully immersed in an international network covering every aspect of the revelations that were happening at a rapid rate. But even though I could calculate and see it on paper, personally I couldn't get it and verbally I couldn't express it. The more I researched, ran programs, looked for keys and triggers, the more depressed I became. In my own sad mind, I questioned, is there a trick to it? Is it false hope or just some kind of much needed dead-end emotional stampede? I was a mess. By Thanksgiving, when my parents visited, I couldn't talk. We suffered in silence the whole time together, and I remember thinking, being dead would be better than this."

Mr. Hal cried out, "I didn't know!" and wept on Miss Janine's shoulder.

"No Dad, It's all good. It wasn't you or Mom, it was something bigger, something none of us understood."

At this point in time, I know there is food on the table, and we've been eating, but by the look on everybody's face, we were all thoroughly drawn into Hal Jr.'s words and we want him to go on.

"Within two weeks of the hijacking, a growing movement called the *forgiveness challenge* started. People challenged themselves to see if through concentration, meditation, or by just saying the words, that they could see the light, find their way, change their life. People were doing it just on a whim and for so many it was working without much effort. It scared me. I couldn't see how it could work. What about the evil and the horrendous? I shook with fear at the places my mind went. Emotionally, I flailed about. While others were making headway, accepting, and experiencing epiphanies, I wrestled with the dark."

He had himself another sip of tea and went on, "December dragged, and I was worse than I'd ever been. My electronic data gathering and dealings with the *total forgiveness* network was ongoing, as was my deep daily depression. Up until the day before Christmas I was completely inert, stolid, immobilized, and unresponsive.

"On that day I went to the cafe just around the corner from where I live. I sat in the front window at a little table and had lunch. The place was busy with people in and out picking up Christmas orders. Then I saw a girl I recognized waiting in line. She lived in the apartment complex I had just moved from in November. I didn't know her well, except maybe that she had anger issues. She was always yelling at someone. As I watched her in line, I vividly remembered the last time we saw each other. It was the end of October, I was moving out and making trips back and forth to my new place when I returned to get some more stuff and there he was, that guy, the reason I was moving, blocking the front door with his dog. He had my number and terrorized me whenever he saw me. The dog was straight out of a late-night horror movie. His jagged pointy teeth set in a mouth wider than his head and oozed a foamy rabid slime. He viciously strained on a too tight barbaric spiked leather collar that was attached to a big heavy chain that the guy cracked on his back to violently antagonize him to git me, all the while yelling, 'What's the matter? Fraid I'll let him loose?' Then he would rattle the chain again and threaten, 'Maybe this dog is gonna getcha.' I couldn't move and with every breath I took, the dog would strain on that chain and growl. I was frozen in fear.

"Then from behind me comes this girl, the one waiting in line, and she yells at the guy in a high-pitched voice, 'What the heck are you doing? Put that damn dog away and stop trying to scare people.' He shook the chain on the dog's back again and started to come at her, but she pointed her finger and yelled, 'You heard me, put that dog away!' And then she grabbed me by the arm and walked me right past them and into the building."

He continued, "I was deep in that memory when I saw her finish her order and come towards me. I wasn't sure what to expect, as I was nervous with any public agitation, but she plunked right down at my table, smiled, and said hi. I noticed right away that she was different. Was it her smile? The ease at which she approached? I kept my eyes down as she spoke. At first, she just made small talk, but then they called out a number for pick up, she looked at her number and said, 'I'll guess I'll be here for a while,' and without missing a beat, she asked if I wanted to hear what happened to her?"

He stopped, took a bite of food, and said, "As always, I didn't know what to say, but I did nod my head, and so she told me this extraordinary story." Pausing he said, "It's a little long and graphic?"

If he was asking us if we wanted to hear it, of course we did. His words had already transported us. We could hardly believe this was Hal Jr. Then using a different voice inflection, he seemed to remember every word she said, and recounted her story as if it were his own. "When I was six my mother's boyfriend moved in with us; my mother, my little brother and me. We lived in a small, dirty, rundown, ram-shackled rental on the outskirts of town. Her boyfriend had a ten-year-old daughter that would come on the weekends. She didn't like me. At first, she just tripped me up, tipped over my drinks, and took my food. When I said I would tell, she threatened to smother me in my sleep, burn me in my bed and kill my little brother. Each weekend it got worse.

"On this particular weekend, my mother and her boyfriend were fighting and yelling like they always did and sent us girls out to the backyard where there was a falling down out building with an old, abandoned refrigerator, the kind with the big handle you have to lift up on to open. Somehow, she forced me into the refrigerator and closed the door. At first it was the absolute darkness that scared me, then I couldn't breath, and soon I was panicked. I remember I had to go to the bathroom and couldn't hold it. My mind emptied and when I could think no more, the door opened, and as the light and air rushed in, she stood there screaming, 'You stink, you wet your pants, I'm telling.' And ran towards the house yelling.

"I drug myself out of the refrigerator and limped to the house, where my mother yelled at me, 'What the hell, look at you!' Her boyfriend put his hands on my shoulders and held me out and away saying, 'What the hell is wrong with you?' I said something like, I'm going to be sick, and he told me he'd give me something to be sick about when, all of a sudden, I threw up all over his pants and shoes. He pushed me backwards and called me disgusting.

My mother screamed at me and apologized to him for having such a disgusting kid and sent me to the room I shared with my brother.

"The yelling went on for a long time, then there was a knock on the front door, and after a few minutes my mother came into our room with some papers in hand and took my brother out of his bed. I asked her what was going on and she said, 'His frickin father is here and wants him, well he can have him.' And within minutes he was gone. I remember begging to hold him one more time, but she wouldn't let me.

"The fight between my mother and her boyfriend went on and later that night he grabbed up his things and his daughter and left. My mother went on a rampage and blamed me for everything. The next morning, I woke up and had wet the bed, which enraged her even more. Everything went downhill from there. I missed my brother so much and I feared the dark that plagued my sleep.

I started to wet the bed every night and my mother would tell her friends that I was a burden child, useless.

"Years went by and no matter how much she humiliated me, I couldn't stop wetting the bed. Sometimes she would make me sleep naked on the floor to teach me a lesson. We moved around quite a bit, I didn't always have a bed and friends of my mother didn't want me sleeping on their couch. We almost never had a washer and dryer and so at school I became known as the stinky girl.

"I couldn't recover. As I got older my mother counted down the years saying, 'I can't wait until you're old enough to get the hell out of here and clean up after yourself, then you'll see what a pain in the ass you are.'

"I quit school at seventeen, got a job in a fast-food restaurant, saved up enough money for the cheapest place to live and moved out. I was so afraid of wetting my new bed I stayed up all night for a week and somehow it just stopped, but within a few days my mother moved out of town, not telling me where, and I was left alone in the world. Almost immediately I got sick, I couldn't seem to hold any food down. I would just bend over and out it would come. I was a basket case, a lonely, scared basket case.

"One day at work after a birthday party there was a large leftover sheet cake. Two girls I worked with were eating a third piece and then going into the bathroom to throw it up. They said they were eating for sport and trying to perfect the art of purging. I thought I can do that without even trying, so I did it for sport, and within the week I was doing it all the time. There was plenty of free food for me at the restaurant and I gorged myself on other people's half-eaten thrown away meals. Once again, I was disgusting.

"For twelve years I was addicted to binge and purge, going from a few times a day to twenty times and that was the state I was in the last time I saw you at the end of October. A dentist who looked in my mouth told me I was going to lose my teeth, my esophagus was going to rot out, and my heart was going to explode. I tried everything but I couldn't stop. There was no discipline, no petition, no plea, that worked. I was a loser. It's not like I wated to die, but I felt I was going to. My whole life had been one big mess after another, I was so far gone, I couldn't even do a simple thing like eat.

"By Thanksgiving I planned, one more time, to end the cycle. Alone, I cooked enough food to feed an army, vowing to bag all the leftovers into meal portions and regulate my intake, but by the end of the day I had eaten and thrown up most of it. My body ached. I was defeated.

"The next day, I was back to the same old thing, ready to go out and get more food, but then I read something on social media about a *forgiveness challenge*. Like almost everybody, I was already familiar with the stories about the woman from the hijacking. It intrigued me and I thought why not. I was standing in my kitchen, when my head filled with flashbacks of that girl who terrorized me years ago and without thinking too much I grabbed onto the concept of the *challenge*. I pictured that girl and thought to myself, she didn't know what she was doing, so I did what the *challenge* suggested, and in my mind, I forgave her, not just for yesterday, but for tomorrow too. Then thinking about my own problems, something made me cry out, 'I can't do this anymore.' Suddenly, I felt a change come over me, like an all-consuming cloud. In that moment I promised to forgive everyone, my mother too, and as I looked up, I visually saw a door open, then a light poured over me, and when I breathed in the air, I knew somehow, for sure, that my lifelong nightmare was over. I was free and this malady that plagued my very existence was gone."

We were all reeling in our seats. It was such a visual story.

Hal Jr. caught his breath and went on. "Just then they called out her number, her order was ready, and she got up. Her story had put me in such a fog, I couldn't think of what to say, so I asked, 'What's going on with that guy and his dog?'

"She said, 'He moved out.'

"I asked her, 'Where'd he go?'

"She said, 'I think he moved to this neighborhood.'

"I choked, fear set in and I'm sure she could see it in my eyes. She went up to get her order and came back by and said, 'I can tell you're freaking out, and you're gonna freak out again, and when you do, remember my story, it's true and it's gonna help.' She touched my hand and out she went.

"Shaken, I left the cafe. The small cottage I lived in was just a short walk away and as I turned the corner to my street, I saw what I was sure, was that guy and his dog down at the end of my street taking a left and going out of sight. I don't think he saw me. I was catatonic at that point. Had he just walked past my house? Does he know where I live? I was struck by a hyperventilating paranoia that seemed to paralyze. How could I live with him near me? The thought crushed any peace, any solace I thought I might have had.

"Somehow, I made it to the gate that opens to my yard and I ran down the newly graveled walkway that leads to a side entrance door. It's a renovated garage, the bedroom is at the front and the main door is all the way down on the left side and opens into a small kitchen living room area. The windows at the back face the morning sun. I had only lived there for a short time and loved it. Now I was filled with dread. How could I go out? What if he sees me? What if he already knows I'm here? I couldn't keep my head together.

"The night went on. I tried to remember her story, but only thought, she was abused, you can overcome abuse, but me, I'm deficit. I'm not complete. There's no hope for me. I thought of what a disappointment I was to my parents. Why was I even born? And so it continued throughout the night. Crying, succumbing to fear and the looming desire of death that comes with it. Why not I thought, they'll get over it and be better off, and for me the pain will finally be over.

"With lights off, curtains pulled, a sick stomach and a fitful sense, I went to bed. At about five in the morning, I awoke to the sound of that guy flinging open my gate, and him and his dog running down the gravel pathway, chain cracking on his back. Within a second and with a big bang he throws open my storm door, and then nothing. I heard nothing. I had sat up halfway in my bed and waited for him to kick the door in, but nothing. I was afraid to breath, sure that he and his dog were just waiting for me to move, to make a sound, and so I stayed motionless for what seemed like eternity. Two hours later, the sun was coming up, I could hear the birds, so with a blanket wrapped around me and over my head I got out of bed and creeped into the kitchen. I was afraid to pull back the curtains, thinking he and that dog were still there, scheming, waiting for me to let my guard down. Finally, something gave me enough nerve and I opened the curtains to expose the morning sun and when I did, I realized that that guy and his dog weren't there, they were never there, it wasn't real, it didn't happen, it was a dream, a vivid shocking dream, and as I squinted at the light of day, I called out for help. A vision of that guy and his dog entered my mind, I embraced them, and in my mind, I made them my friends and like a brother I would forgive no matter what. Then I saw my parents and the pain they would live with if I were to die. My body filled with empathy and compassion overtook my reason. I promised to live and then suddenly there was a large lighted carousel above me, and it was coming around and I knew all I had to do was reach up and I did."

With that he stopped talking for a second, looked at all of us with our mouths open and the sound of our hearts beating hard, and told us with such gentleness, "When I reached up, I knew immediately, I was all better."

Miss Janine cried out for joy more than a couple of times and there were tears streaming down Mr. Hal's face. My mouth was dry. The whole story was incredible. Mr. Clarke didn't say anything, but was breathing normally, as opposed to not. Janie, at first, looked pale, hunched over, but when Jack got up and affectionately stood behind her and put his hands on his shoulders, her body language changed, she put her shoulders back, and a soft smile came across her face. And because he could hardly wait to know more and if thirst had a picture, it would be Uncle David's face, and so, he asked the question, "What on God's earth do you think is going on?"

Hal Jr. gave answers, brave and bold, saying, "The end to all violence is close at hand, inevitable, airborne, and highly communicable. It's a dimension we've only had an inkling about, and now it's showing us how to achieve it, by revealing a path and benefits not thought possible." Then pointing to himself, said, "Just look at me." He then went on to use words like "classic multiplication, no downside, a time without malice, and a home that feeds all,. . . our destiny."

I got lost in my own thoughts for a minute when I saw Miss Janine catching my attention and pointing to the kitchen. I got up and followed her in. She had a small birthday cake, we put one candle on it and came out singing. The levity was good. Uncle David raised his glass and toasted to "Henry Allen Lee Jr."

But Miss Janine ran her hand across her face with her index finger swaying back and forth, shaking her head no, and said, "He's not Henry Allen, he's Henry Angel Lee. Angel is his middle name. He's a Hal, he's just not a junior."

There was a lot of wow talk about it and everyone ate their cake. I helped Miss Janine take the dishes back into the kitchen and that's when I asked her how it came to be that Henry got Angel for a middle name. She said, "Before Henry, I had two late term miscarriages. I was scared to get pregnant again, but we wanted to have a child and so with a lot of trepidation, I did. Six months into the pregnancy we were in the middle of buying a home. Our agent was a great person, she could see I was uptight and asked what was wrong. I told her of my past, my fear of losing another child, and my guilt about what happened to the souls of the little ones that didn't live.

"The next time we met, our agent brought me a paperback booklet and told me it contained different readings from a psychic that died in the 1940's. She said he was asked a lot of deep questions when he was in a trance, and here was one she wanted me to read. I took the booklet from her and read the question: When does a soul enter the body? At conception or at birth? And his answer was, at birth.

"It was unreal how much it relieved me, my guilt, and my fear. I took it to heart. Then on New Year's Eve when I was eight months pregnant, I went into labor. There was concern for our health and I was sedated. At first, I panicked, then I saw an apparition, like a video I'd seen years ago, taken in an old hotel by an infrared ghost camera. It resembled a small human shape, lighted, moving just a little bit, and it sat in the air just above me. I swore it told me I had 'nothing to fear.' When they said push, I closed my eyes and pushed. I opened them to see Henry take his first breath. I looked around and it was gone, but I was sure what I had seen, and I had no doubt about what it was. A soul in waiting, his guardian angel." Shaking she took a deep breath and said, "Except for Hal, I've never told that story to anyone."

They were calling out to us from the other room, she hugged me, and we walked back into the mix. Uncle David was saying, "I can't believe it, with the storm and all, I almost turned around and didn't come tonight." He was beside himself with joy and kept saying things like, "What a night! What a wonderful night!"

It was just after eleven, the snow was slowing down, and Miss Janine wanted to get her two Hals home before midnight. Mr. Hal was still crying and insisted on hugging every one of us before he left. Miss Janine was steady, clearly on top of the world, and Hal Jr. radiated like a warm friend, who had come home to lend a hand.

As we walked them to the door, wishing Happy New Year and Happy Birthday, we were all in agreement to meet right back here in this very room at ten in the morning. Something was going on and we were sure we had just caught a glimpse.

Mr. Clarke looked brighter, but not over-the-moon affected by Hal Jr., not personally, as if he couldn't absorb it, and because of that, Jack and Janie remained quiet. Uncle David on the other hand was as high-as-a-kite and said he would love to spend the midnight hour by himself, in his room, if that was okay? And I wanted to do the same. Mr. Clarke wished us a good night and bid us to go on up. Then he put his arms around Jack and Janie and gave us an unexpected heartfelt thank you for being his friend and sticking with him.

As I headed to my room, I thought, what a turning point this was. Since the hijacking we've read so many stories. Now to see it so dramatically in Hal Jr., and then to watch it affect his parents in a such a quick and cascading manner, I was glowing inside, amazed at everything. I didn't know exactly what was going on, but it sure seemed that some subtle breeze of the most-gentlest kind was here in our midst, and it was shifting us, and I liked it.

AS ONE

Last night was such a hot rush of information that our horizons expanded beyond set-in-stone logic. I wondered how much of what Hal Jr. said took root and how much, like the fast-pace of mini-episodes, would it explode exponentially?

We woke to the New Year knowing the dynamics had clearly and dramatically changed. Jack and Janie looked relatively rested. Uncle David was perfectly collected, serene. It seemed his demeanor now suited his calling. Mr. Hal was a different person altogether, altered in such a visual way. The sharpness of his persona, his every edge, smoothed over, and his expression was that of someone who had held a new born baby for the first time. Miss Janine blossomed. Her eyes no longer looked inward but boasted open with invites to see and grasp her gratitude and be her joy. Hal Jr. was ready, surrounded by everything he had hoped to have, family, friends, and a shared reason.

Mr. Clarke, the last to arrive at breakfast, looked lighted, almost translucent, and with such sincerity said to Hal Jr., "I've been humbled. The stories you told and your undeniable recovery shook things in me I didn't know existed." Pointing to Jack and Janie, "The kids and I stayed up after midnight and talked for a bit. I was deeply affected, but I still felt impenetrable and went to bed filled with questions, still unforgiveable and lost."

Hal Jr. tried to jump in and say, "Mr. Clarke, no, I didn't mean to make you...."

But Mr. Clarke cut him off, looked at everyone and spilled out, "What I want to tell you all is, I dreamt about my brother last night. I saw him so clear, his eyes squinting, sunlight splashing off his face. So close I could smell his aftershave, and when I did, it transported me to where I thought he was going to reach out and pull me close. I was young and I remember crossing over into another place, as if he was right there."

Miss Janine said, "Oh John, I'm so happy for you."

Hal Jr. said, "From all the data, most everyone has dream-oriented progress. The suppression of dreams by depreciation or casting their value as optional is ending. What we surmise, is that our bodies are occupied with a force, from the moment we're born to the moment we die; and our dreams provide as many answers as does the day. It's ethereal, the next level, where we start to see where we come from, our purpose on earth, and where exactly we go, what form we take, and what communication we make when we pass away. It's an understandable system."

Of course, once again, our eyes were spinning in our heads.

Mr. Clarke said exuberantly, "Bring it on Henry! I need to hear as much as you can say. After last night's interview, I'm sure I'm going to have to brief the media today and it'll be better with the more I know."

The first order of business was for everyone to watch the video of the visit between Christopher's aunt and Mr. Clarke on Christmas Eve. The mood became somber, there was crying. Mr. Clarke's wrenching past, writhing regret, and wringing wet tears reminded us of how weary his warped situation had become.

But when Christopher's aunt said, 'I would smile, call you brother, and tell stories to rouse you from the fence,' everyone was rapt. The way she strung her words together, as if weightless, and when she said, 'places where vibrant life forms, such as forgiveness and compassion are complete and vengeance isn't even a word,' Hal Jr. went wild. He was gasping for breath and our sensibilities were rocked with alternative possibilities of levels just starting to show themselves.

We skipped lunch to spend more time going over the words of Christopher's aunt, the enormity of the intense astronomical changes experienced by so many with this *forgiveness thing*, and what to say at the news conference scheduled for three o'clock in the White House Briefing Room. Hal Jr. gave Mr. Clarke a short list of points to keep him on track.

It was quarter after two when Mr. Clarke decided to go to his room, just to rest for a few minutes, gather himself, maybe read some personal mail that had been building up. He hadn't been gone for more than five minutes when he returned holding a letter and an envelope. He looked like he'd been struck in the head and shouted, "Look at this, I can't believe it." We gathered around as he read the letter.

Dear Mr. President,

I am a retired Army officer. My military career was stellar, but my personal life fell short. My young teenage granddaughter, a light in my life, had taken to bad times and dangerous activities. I found myself screaming at the water's edge, begging for her to catch a glimpse, but things got worse, so much so, that in all my days, I had never felt so helpless.

And then on Christmas Eve she called and said, "Papa, I'm all better." I could hear it in her voice, something extraordinary had happened. The next day, Christmas, she visited, and I witnessed the amazing change first-hand.

She spoke of this *forgiveness challenge* thing and how she did it on a whim with some of her friends. I asked her if I could help her with anything and she replied, "Yes, Papa, can you stop being so angry?"

I served three tours in Vietnam and had boxed all my memories. Later that night, conflicted, I went to the attic and opened them up. I used to take pictures of the new guy's first day in-country and thought you might want this one.

The guy all the way to the right, kneeling down, that's your brother. Turn it over, see where I marked it, some got nicknames right away. We called your brother Angel because he was like an Angel. I thought you might like to know.

With tears streaming down his face, Mr. Clarke cried, "It was just how I saw him in my dream, how does that happen? What's going on?" Jack and Janie hugged on him. Mr. Clarke cried again, "But where's my wife? Where's your mother?" Then hugging back on his kids, he looked up and wept in agony saying, "I'm sorry. Forgive me. I love you and I'll do anything just to see you one more time."

It was emotional, point on, and draining but with just minutes before the news briefing, Mr. Clarke had to pull himself together, and all the while clutching his brother's picture.

Mr. Hal took the podium to introduce President Clarke, but before he could say much, he was bombarded with questions and ended up responding in a plea-filled manner, "I was wrong when I called it nonsense."

Someone yelled, "So you're flip-flopping? Changing your mind?"

Somberly he replied, "I'm not flip-flopping. I didn't change my mind." Then he paused and said shakingly, "Most of you have known me and my family for years. Something's going on. I've been changed. My whole family has been changed. Outside in? Inside out? I can't understand it, but

I know it, I'm changed, I've been changed." He stood tall and his eyes welled-up.

Someone else yelled, "Is it that woman? Can you at least confirm the rumor that she met with the President on Christmas Eve?"

And before he could catch himself, he blurted out, "Yes, she visited him on Christmas Eve." And then deferred to Mr. Clarke apologetically for answering the question.

President Clarke came out to a fury of shouts. One by one they probed the strangest scenarios or asked the oddest things like, "What are you going to do about these so-called forgivers? Aren't they out of their minds? It's just silly, everything they advocate goes against everything we hold dear. This forgiveness thing is an affront to our judicial system. Do you really think people want to give up the right to judge others? Don't you know that by giving them an inch, you're pandering to an illusion that thinks it can eliminate violence and that's just unreal, an imagination gone wild. People want people to pay the price. We've got prisons and hell for one reason, to put the bad ones away."

It was brutal. He asked them to, "Simmer down, nobody is forcing anybody to give up anything." And then he went on sarcastically, "I was asked, what if those so-called forgivers want to sweet talk themselves into believing they can change the world one person at a time, and I thought, what if they try? What can they do? Change the world?"

That got their ire up even more. They almost booed him. Someone yelled out, "Mr. President, I heard they don't use the word god. They're talking about some higher power, some blanket thing, in my book, that's blasphemy."

Mr. Clarke paused and said, "What if I were to ask you right now what your god looks like? Really? Could you tell me? What if I asked everyone here today, what's your god look like? Got a robe? Long hair? Sitting in a big chair and holding a big staff? Would it be a gender? Would it float in the air? Would it be different for each one of us? And would it all be subject to change if we only had more information?"

"But Sir, they have a notion of a world without borders, one community, seriously, isn't that completely absurd?"

"I say, what if children with food, water, shelter, affection, education and safety could wake up every morning without anxiety because they know that everyone, in our world, is working together making sure that every child has those basic things?"

"Oh, come on now Mr. President, in this country we value our defense system and our right to seek justice, this is a huge mechanism that cannot be broken down by a bunch of naïve people thinking we can take care of everyone, it's not realistic. We elected you as our President, you can't just go and change what's always been."

"First of all, change is not mine to meter out and what if it's a change whose time has come? What if it's a fact and unstoppable? Bigger than we know?"

"Sir, let's be clear, there's always been and always will be threats and the horror of death and we can't survive without the ability to retaliate and show them we mean business."

"Well then let me be even clearer still, what if it's over? What if people killing people is over? What if there's no more benefit? What if turning the cheek is our only move? What if, because of that, the threats that multiply fear and instill insanity disappear? What if the resources used for destruction are used for good? What if we never saw another commercial showing a starving baby, because there were no more starving babies? And what if we understood our interdependence on a level only dreamed about?"

The man fired back, "I'm sorry sir but I think you're freakin crazy!" Then he threw down his notebook and stormed out.

It was a knock down drag out. There was no rhyme or reason to the volley, and the defense of death as retaliation, or for gain, was relentless. Mr. Clarke spoke from his gut and handled all they could throw at him. Right at the end, the Christmas Eve visit from that woman, was brought up and Mr. Clarke volunteered, that with Christopher's aunt's permission, he would release the video immediately. The briefing concluded and stunned we all met back in the private quarters of the White House.

Before any mention of what just took place, Mr. Clarke called Christopher's aunt and put her on speaker phone. We all said hey and she said hey back. He advised her their visit was revealed and he wanted to release it. She laughed and asked, "Was it Hal?"

Mr. Hal moved in close to the phone and said, "Yes Mam, it was me."

You could hear a smile in her voice, "Oh good, and yes, certainly you can release it."

Mr. Clarke thanked her, and she asked him, "Have you seen anyone?"

He answered, "Yes, my brother, twice today."

She replied, "Oh, so glad to hear." and then wished us a good night.

With a flick of a finger the video of their visit was released to the public and the wires already hot with the intense briefing banter caught wind and permeated more senses than had ever been counted before. The briefing broadcasted live was replayed and replayed in every language. Within the hour the visit video was released, and people could not stop watching it. Around the globe, the discussion brought more people together than could have been realized. The air waves were maxing out. Everything at the White House was off the hook.

Mr. Clarke turned to Hal Jr. and asked, "Henry, what do we do next?"

Hal Jr. said, "I think we lay low and come up with a plan."

"Shouldn't I explain something? I think I was rambling quite a bit out there and that video of me with Christopher's aunt, shouldn't I say something?"

"No, you don't need to say anything. There's enough people talking about what just happened and what they're seeing, and by the way, at the briefing, you did a great job, you were definitely all over the board, but you did a great job."

Mr. Clarke smiled and thanked him, "So, what do you think we should do?"

Hal Jr. replied, "I think we should change our focus from something we can't do much about, to something we can. I'm thinking Inauguration Day. It's a little over two weeks away and I have an idea."

We were all ears, we talked, we brainstormed, we ate, we built excitement and tried to give it form. By the end of the night, we had envisioned pulling off, some kind of, All-Inclusive Worldwide Communication Modern Day Marvel. Hal Jr. laughed and said, "Now all we need is a theme and a song, Mrs. Clarke would love it."

We all agreed, but it was clear by the blue look on his face, that Mr. Clarke filled with melancholy at the mention of Mrs. Clarke. We ran late into the evening and finished knowing we would have to be ready to start first thing in the morning.

I went to bed with my mind racing like an open can of worms. The story behind the Clarke family, the one I have kept to myself, was now out there, revealed to everyone. The nightmares, the heartache, the tragedy, all revealed to everyone, in one fell swope. I could hardly wrap my head around the fact that there were no more secrets to keep. My boss sent a thumbs up and I felt a freeing sensation, like a weight being lifted. I simmered down and choose to embrace my time for sleep. Tomorrow would be here soon enough.

The next morning, January 2nd, the world was a buzz with "what ifs" and surprisingly, a lot of empathy and solidarity. There were the die-hards preaching doom and gloom, threatening force, and drastic measures, but honestly, they didn't seem as loud as I would have thought. Outside the White House, the dialogue about the briefing and the visit was off the charts. People all over the world, sick of pervasive violence, were choosing to take the *forgiveness challenge* just on principle. People became emotional about the plight of President Clarke and his family and most were mesmerized by Christopher's aunt's choice of words, and as would be expected, there were hundreds of thousands of avenues of speculation. They called it the apocalypse in reverse, the pandemic without a virus, the addiction you don't have to quit, and the end of the world as we know it, and although we all wanted to hash it over with our morning coffee, Hal Jr. was ready for us to focus.

With the first words out of his mouth, Hal Jr. did not disappoint, and as he said them, he had them flash across the big screen in the living room, "Imagine: One Day, One Voice, As One." Pausing he looked at all of us and said, "This will be billed as the largest sing along in history, the most people ever to vocalize at the same time. Today we will put the call out for volunteers around the globe to help facilitate the timing and the technology. We will find a way to fund and deliver the hardware to the remotest people on the planet, and we will coordinate simultaneous two-way transmission, for everyone on Inauguration Day."

The idea was huge, and he went on to say, "We need to put it out there today, preferably this morning. While everyone is talking about yesterday, we need to ride the coat tails of the immense press activity and show everyone what they can do in the near future to be a part of this growing conversation." Pausing he asked, "And how do they do that? By participating in this vast coming together of as many people as can be gathered on earth at one time to sing and to sing until we have literally and metaphorically increased the timber and raised the roof."

Brilliant was the word that came to my mind. We were all in. Before noon, the Imagine plan was released to the world and we were on the pressured countdown to pull it off.

Everything was broken into segments. Mr. Hal was to handle all incoming from military and judiciary. Uncle David was given the spiritual, ecclesiastic input. Miss Janine was following up on astronomical and new age explanations. Mr. Clarke was working the phones with political and media legends. Janie and I organized the singers in the United States, while Jack and Hal Jr. used their influences to expand international approvals and participation. Time was of the essence and after just one day of this project, it seemed like twenty. But by the next day we had volunteers stepping up to the plate and we could see things getting done.

One by one contributors of all sizes came forward to offer all they could in support of the Imagine effort. Before we knew it, we had amassed more than ten times the projected budget. From hardware, software, shipping, and handling, all was paid for. Volunteers organized where they lived. Activists, poets, and philanthropists carved genuine paths through the rhetoric, made resting places in the zones of safety, and helped redefine the door to our new awakening perceptions.

Like the hijacker letting up on his knife, tough leaders gave some way, hard lines grew soft, and openings were made. Spiritual leaders readjusted their allegiances, joined together over church walls, and guided with globality. It was a time of possibilities, and a pep rally for dreams.

Even the media guy that called Mr. Clarke, 'freakin crazy' had an epiphany and apologized. There were so many stories like his, we couldn't keep track.

In such a short time the Imagine project was well underway. A fun mantra had manifested out there, "Imagine, if everybody wins, nobody loses."

Tens of thousands volunteered, a completely wireless system was being set up and it was estimated over half the people of the world could be involved on Inauguration Day. Spectacular numbers.

The next two weeks went by so quick. I had no time for personal reflection. There were so many theories out there, Hal Jr. wanted us to stay focused on the Imagine project and not be pulled into discussions or debates, saying there'll be plenty of time for that after Inauguration Day. People organized and throngs were coming into the Washington area just to sing. Around the globe plans were made to gather in stadiums, town halls, schools, and parks. Big screens popped-up everywhere. People would sing where they worked.

Outside the White House the dialogue continued to fuel itself, as millions more seemed to be affected by this *forgiveness challenge*. Inside the White House we were a well-oiled machine, except for Mr. Clarke. Even though he saw his brother, twice, he hadn't seen his wife. His senses seemed to go dormant. He was trying to write his speech but couldn't build a fire for it.

Early on Inauguration Day Janie and I were scheduled to meet and greet some of the singers at the White House in appreciation for their participation. Janie thanked them for coming, hoped they were finding everything satisfactory, and then asked if they had any questions. One woman raised her hand and asked modestly, "I know you're busy, I sent you an email, but I don't know if you got it? It was a video of your mom singing when she was in high school?"

Janie leaned in and said, "Excuse me? What did you say?"

The woman who was about our age replied, "My mother and your mother were in high school together, they sang in the Octette that travelled with the Dance Band. It was just a short film of your mother singing at a school function. My grandparents were in the audience and took the video."

"No," said Janie, "I didn't see it." And then walked closer to the woman and said, "I'd love to see it, are you sure you sent it to the right address?"

The woman pulled out her phone and resent it. We were amazed at what we saw and couldn't wait to show everyone, especially Mr. Clarke, who we knew was waiting for a sign.

Janie called everyone to the living room and brought it up on the big screen. It was an old grainy clip transferred from an antiquated VCR tape, shot from about three rows back in a high school auditorium. It was the end of the song, the Octettes were swaying in the background for a young Mrs. Clarke, who was singing the lead, and out of her mouth came the song, "*Imagine all the people living life in peace, you may say I'm a dreamer, but I'm not the only one, I hope someday you'll join us, and the world will live as one.*"

There was loud applause, the camcorder jumped around a bit, and you could hear the woman's grandmother whisper to her grandfather, "She sings like an angel."

The grandfather replies loudly, "What?"

And the grandmother whispers again, "She sings like an angel."

Jack was sobbing and Janie held him. Miss Janine hugged on Mr. Hal and said so sweetly,

"She loved her John Lennon." Nodding yes, Uncle David wept.

Mr. Clarke cried out, "It's Mom, she's here."

Yes, she was. It was an Inauguration Day miracle and what a validation for Hal Jr. who had picked the theme. Mrs. Clarke was in the house, all was right with the world, and we were ready to do the day.

To keep it simple, most of the fanfare and tradition of the day's activities were not being done, leaving room for a clear focus on the Imagine project. Around the globe, in every time zone, in every happy and in every most horrific type of situation, people were getting ready to login.

We all gathered at the Capitol. Looking out there was an endless sea of people. Mr. Hal, Miss Janine, Hal Jr., and us kids sat together. Andrew was with us, invited by Mr. Clarke and Christopher attended as my guest. His aunt and her husband were invited; however, they were still on their extended vacation until the end of January and couldn't make it. Mr. Clarke's parents were there, as were my parents.

I had told my father ahead of time, we are going to be on the world stage, so no funny business. When he and my mother arrived, they approached and greeted Mr. Clarke's parents. I watched as my father glanced over his shoulder at me, winked, and then turned to Mr. Clarke's mother, opened the lapel on his jacket and secretively showed her something. There was delight in her eyes and she reached out and hugged him. I couldn't see what it was, but I was sure he had a made ka-pow badge especially for her. Mr. Hal caught a glimpse of what was going on, smiled, and gave my father a thumbs up.

Uncle David gave the blessing, asked people to raise their hands and bow their heads, and said, "With all the planets that surround us, how grateful we are to have this one. A world where everything grows, water flows, and the air is clean. A home where our thoughts expand to solve the tests of time. A fruitful place unlike any other we've encountered. And so, we give thanks for the bounty we receive; and we humbly accept the challenge to share unconditionally all we have forever and ever." There was a moment of silence and then a release as if you could feel the crowd exhale.

Mr. Clarke stood, acknowledged his parents, friends, children, and his other children. We all smiled and he addressed the world.

"Can we imagine living life in peace? Three months ago, I said what most of us said, this is nonsense, can't happen, but then something did. It happened to so many at such a fast pace we were all taken by surprise. Intangible connections are being made and suddenly choices unlike any we have ever been offered present themselves. Do we choose to go down fighting, throwing our children under the bus, and onto the front line of horror, or do we breathe in this new forgiving air of change and choose again?

"Today we raise our hopes together in song. Children who live this day will, in years, tell other children about the sound and the elevation. How voices lifted so high that borders were erased, and fear dissolved; and how our memories, in time, so rich with every sweet cliché of the day, will remind us again and again, that we are the world, this is us, and we want to live as one."

The crowd went wild.

He pointed to me and continued, "I once said to a young friend, there's nothing silly about peace, you just have to give it a chance, so that's what we're going to do." Then turning to the choir, he gave the signal, and they started to sing,

All we are saying is give peace a chance.

Everyone joined in, everyone swooned, it went on for hours, throughout the night, along with thousands of other songs, sung in every known language. Unity. Millions growing to billions gathered to sing. The visuals were stunning. From refugee camps, to prisons, to homeless shelters; from the icy tundra, to the dense jungle, to the inner city and the lonely town; more and more logged in and sang out. The intense and constant crescendo rocked the ethers, and by the next day, collectively, we knew we were going to be *all better.*

ABOUT THE AUTHOR

First time author and longtime optimist, S.T. Stetka, affectionately called Sandra Tracey by her mother, has been talking her story and writing this book for over twenty years. Most wondered if she would ever finish, and if she did, would it be any good?

Undaunted, a contented older hippie, happy wife, sister, and friend, Sandra Tracey ambitiously aimed for the sky with her rich original plot about how peace wins and violence ends.

When the book was finished, she read it to her husband, who at some parts welled up, and then asked her to read it again.